LOVE IN LANCASTER COUNTY

BEYOND PRICE

· Barbara Cameron ·

Annie's®

Books in the Love in Lancaster County series

Library of Congress-in-Publication Data
Beyond Price / by Barbara Cameron
p. cm.
I. Title
                                    2021946709

AnniesFiction.com
(800) 282-6643
Love in Lancaster County™
Series Creator: Shari Lohner

10 11 12 13 14 | Printed in South Korea | 9 8 7 6 5 4 3 2 1

For Eva and Donna

Note: Although there are many similarities among Amish communities around the country, each community makes its own rules. The Lancaster County, Pennsylvania, Amish community allows cell phones, whereas some other Amish communities limit or ban them.

Who can find a virtuous woman? For her price is far above rubies.

—Proverbs 31:10

CHAPTER ONE

Ruby Beiler rushed into her bedroom. She was running late, and she'd promised Sarah she'd show up early for the evening's singing and help with the refreshments.

Quickly, she pulled off the kerchief and house dress she'd worn while cleaning and cooking and watching a *Boppli* on the one day she had off from her job at a shop in town. Her *Schweschder* had left her Boppli with Ruby and her *Mudder* while she went to a doctor's appointment. Ruby didn't mind. She loved taking care of the Boppli and the house.

She brushed out her long brown hair, frowning at her reflection in the mirror over her dresser. Brown hair, brown eyes. *Drab,* she thought. *Mousey.* Her Schweschder had gotten their Mudder's wheat-blonde hair and blue eyes.

She looked in her closet and debated which of the two Sunday dresses she owned she would wear tonight. Since she'd worn the dove-gray one to church that morning, she pulled on the green one. The trouble was, it was starting to show some wear. She hadn't loved the drab olive color when she bought it, but the fabric had been on sale. With a sigh, she pulled it on anyway.

She opened the little wooden keepsake box on the dresser and pulled out a pile of hairpins. After she parted her hair in the middle and drew it back, she twisted it and used the pins to secure a neat bun at the nape of her neck. Then she topped her head with a sheer white starched *Kapp*.

With one finger, she traced her name painted on the top of the keepsake box. *Ruby.* Her name had never felt right to her. A ruby was a jewel, something beautiful and exotic. She'd seen one in an *Englisch* jewelry store window once. It sparkled in the sunlight that hit it and glowed rich and red. On the box, a red plastic imitation stone was glued at the end of the name.

There was nothing beautiful or exotic or even red about her.

When Ruby had asked her mother about her name, she'd just shrugged and said she'd always liked it and that it was the name of a great-aunt. And did she want to be named something plain?

Well, yes, she'd have liked that, but since her mother had been frowning when she asked the question, Ruby didn't say so.

With another sigh, she left the room. She really didn't want to stand out with her name or her appearance. She just wanted to be prettier and have clothes that weren't so worn.

Then she chided herself. She hadn't been raised to believe that physical appearance was important. She straightened her shoulders and walked downstairs, telling herself that she was going to the singing to be with friends, to raise her voice in song and praise and enjoy the evening—not to focus on herself.

"I hitched up the buggy for you," her *Dat* said as he poured himself a cup of coffee.

"Thanks, *Daed*."

"It's a nice evening for a singing," her mother said, looking up from mending a dress. "But it'll be a little chilly later. Take your sweater."

Ruby took it from the peg by the door and picked up her purse. She was grown, but her Mudder still worried about such things.

"Have fun," Miriam said with a smile.

"I will."

"I remember asking if I could drive you home after a singing," she heard her Dat saying as she opened the kitchen door to leave. "*Schur* am glad I did."

"Me too," her Mudder said as Ruby closed the door.

Her *Eldres* didn't say such things often, but when they did, it warmed her heart so. They made her long for a relationship like theirs.

Sometimes she wondered if she was going to be *En Alt Maedel.* Then she shook her head at such silliness. Amish Maedels were getting married later, just like Englisch ones. Twenty-two was *not* old enough to start thinking she was going to remain unmarried.

Spring in Lancaster County was cool—even chilly—but already there were signs of the season as she guided her family's buggy down the lane. Buds were appearing on trees, daffodils and crocuses gave a splash of color, and spring planting had begun.

Ruby stopped the buggy in front of her *Aenti*'s house. She stepped out, a basket over her arm, and saw Leah sitting on the front porch with her hands folded in her lap. Leah was in her sixties and, like Ruby's Mudder, was slender and fine-boned. As Ruby climbed the front steps, she studied Leah's face and thought it looked older, more tired than it had earlier that day at church.

"I wasn't expecting you," Leah said, setting aside a sketch pad and pencil.

"*Mamm* wanted me to drop some food by for you," Ruby told her, setting the basket down on the table between the two rocking chairs. She was running late but wanted to make sure that everything was *allrecht.*

"Miriam's such a worrier," Leah said. "I told her I fixed my supper."

"Well then, you can put this in the refrigerator for tomorrow's lunch."

"I made some fresh lemonade if you want it."

Ruby shook her head. *"Nee, Danki.* I promised I'd help Sarah with refreshments at the singing."

"Then you'd best be on your way so that you won't be late."

Ruby's hand flew to her mouth, and she felt distressed. "Oh, I didn't mean I had to rush off—"

Leah patted her hand. "I know. But you should be going; spend some time with young people. You're always helping everyone. Go have some fun."

"There's plenty of time for that. Mamm said the two of you went to the doctor the other day, and you had some tests."

"Haven't heard anything yet. I don't expect any problems. It's just old age creeping up."

"You're not old," Ruby told her emphatically.

Leah chuckled. "Well, I'm feeling it. Now go on, and we'll talk another day."

"If you insist," Ruby said, throwing up her hands as if in protest. She got out of her chair and leaned down to kiss her Aenti's weathered cheek. "I'll come over and help you clean tomorrow. We'll have what's in the basket for lunch. Mamm packed some brownies I made for the singing."

"Oh?" Leah lifted the lid on the basket and peeked inside. "Those might not be here the next time you come."

"Then I'll just have to bake some more tomorrow while I'm here." She started for the stairs. "See you tomorrow, dear one."

"You're the dear one," Leah responded cheerfully. "Drive carefully."

Ruby thought it was a *gut* thing that buggy horses didn't need a driver's attention because as she passed the home of Leah's handsome neighbor, a *Wittmann,* she was distracted by seeing him sitting on his porch, brooding out at the road.

Daniel Fisher had just walked out of his house, intending to check on Leah, his next-door neighbor, when he saw a buggy pull up in front of her house and Ruby, one of her nieces, get out.

He usually checked on Leah about this time of day since she was getting up in years and not in the best health lately. But because she had a visitor, he decided to hold off until she was alone. Her visitor was one he knew from her frequent visits, a shy, quiet Maedel who'd been a couple of years behind him in *Schul*. He took a seat in one of the rocking chairs on his porch as he watched her hurry up the stairs to Leah's.

While he couldn't hear their conversation, he could see that the two women seemed to be at odds. Ruby looked concerned, but Leah kept shaking her head and appeared to be disagreeing with her. Finally, Ruby threw up her hands as if giving up, bent to kiss Leah's cheek, then hurried back out to her buggy and left.

He got up, strolled over to Leah's, and climbed the stairs.

"Daniel! You just missed Ruby," she said. "Do you have time to sit for a bit?"

He nodded and took a seat. "My Mudder will be bringing the *Kinna* back in a little while. She had them over for a visit this afternoon after church."

"If she'd kept them a little longer, you could have gone to the singing."

"Too old for that sort of thing."

"Now, Daniel, I know how old you are," she chided. "Don't be acting like you're your Dat's age."

"Let's just say singings are for people younger than me. Those interested in marriage." He kept his gaze on the road in front of them, not wanting to see the sympathy in her eyes.

"It's been nearly two years," she said quietly. "Sadie would want you to have a *Fraa*, a Mudder for your Kinna."

"You've been a *Wittfraa* for longer," he pointed out, then wished he'd kept his words to himself as a look of pain crossed her face. "I'm sorry. I shouldn't have said such a thing."

She shook her head. "It's allrecht. It's true. I'm not looking to get married again at my age. You, on the other hand, have your whole life ahead of you. Remember, it says in the Bible it's not *gut* for the man to be alone. That's why He created Eve. We're better together than we are alone."

"You sound like Isaac," he told her.

"I figure I know the Bible about as well as the bishop," she said with a bit of tartness in her voice. "I'm a *gut* twenty years older than him."

She sighed. "Let's not talk about age. Ruby was fussing at me just now, asking about the doctor and offering to help me around the house."

"What did the doctor have to say about you feeling so tired lately?" he asked quietly. "You did keep your appointment the other day, didn't you?"

She nodded. "He had his nurse take a lot of blood from my arm. And he's scheduled me for some tests at the hospital later this week."

They sat and watched a line of buggies traveling down the road in front of the house.

"Lots of young people going to the singing tonight," she said.

Daniel rolled his eyes. "Not that again, Mamm."

She swatted him on the arm. "There comes your Mudder now," she said as a buggy pulled up in front of his house. "Bet she'd say the same thing I did. That you need to get out there with young people your age, think about getting married again."

When the buggy stopped, two Kinna scrambled out, giggling.

"I'm over here!" Daniel called out to them, and they ran to join him on Leah's porch.

"*Daedi*! We had fun at *Grossmudder*'s house!" Eight-year-old Mary beamed at him. She was the image of her late Mudder, with her honey-blonde hair and blue eyes.

"*Grossdaadi* is so silly," six-year-old Samuel told him, climbing up into Daniel's lap. He had a hint of auburn in his brown hair, like Daniel, and hazel eyes. And he was already showing signs he was going to be as tall as his Dat.

"He made us puppets and talked like this." He lowered his high *Kinner*'s voice and made rumbly noises in his throat.

"And Grossmudder said I didn't have to take a nap today," Mary piped up.

"Which is why Grossmudder is exhausted," Waneta said as she climbed the stairs well behind them. "Hello, Leah." She turned to Daniel. "What are you feeding these Kinna to give them so much energy?"

"Vegedabbles," Samuel complained and sighed heavily. "Too many vegedabbles."

"Vegetables," Daniel corrected. "They help you grow and give you strong bones."

"So that's why they outran me when we played in the yard." Waneta leaned against the porch railing, looking like she needed propping up.

"Here, sit, Mamm," Daniel said, standing up and offering her his chair.

She shook her head. "If I sit, I might not get up again, and I need to get home. The Kinna ate supper, so you don't need to feed them." She turned to Leah. "I'll see you later this week at the sewing circle."

"Wouldn't miss it for the world."

Waneta hugged Mary and Samuel, kissed Daniel on the cheek, and then left them.

"Well, time to take these two home for their baths and get them to bed," Daniel told Leah. "Is there anything you need before we go?"

She shook her head. "See you all tomorrow."

As they walked the short distance to their house, Samuel tugged on Daniel's hand. "Daedi, I'm *hungerich*."

"You had supper at Grossmudder's house," he reminded his *Sohn*.

He rolled his eyes. "That was hours and hours ago."

Daniel knew it had been an hour or two at most but also knew his Sohn was a growing boy and a bottomless pit. Resigned, he told them to head into the kitchen and wash their hands. Going to the refrigerator, he pulled out a block of cheese and a dish of butter, then put a cast-iron skillet on the stove.

"Grilled cheese sandwiches and Three Bear Soup coming up," he said, earning a smile from Mary. She loved grilled cheese sandwiches.

"It's vegedabble soup," Samuel said with disgust. "Bears wouldn't eat it."

Daniel sighed inwardly. His late Fraa had always called vegetable soup Three Bear Soup and told the Kinna a story as they ate it, warning them to be careful it wasn't too hot, too cold, but just right when they dipped in their spoons.

He thought of her as the three of them sat at the big kitchen table and ate without her.

CHAPTER TWO

"I'm so sorry I'm late." Ruby rushed up to Sarah with the container of brownies she'd baked for the singing. "I had to make a stop along the way."

"Anything wrong?" Sarah asked as she dumped a bag of potato chips into a big plastic bowl. "You look a little worried."

Ruby shook her head. "Mamm wanted me to drop off some food at Leah's house. She's been feeling a little tired lately."

"I'm schur she's fine. She's always charging about, keeping busy."

Ruby nodded. "I hope so." She glanced around as several buggies pulled into the driveway of the house. "We have a lot of people coming tonight."

"Hope we have enough snacks," Sarah said with a frown. "Ruby?"

"Hmm?" Ruby was distracted. Isaiah Miller had just arrived, and she watched as he walked across the lawn. She'd always thought he was so *gut*-looking, with his blue eyes and dark-blond hair. He smiled, and she felt her heart skip a beat. Actually felt her heart skip a beat. She smiled. He was going to stop and talk to her, really talk to her.

And then he walked right past her. When she recovered and looked after him, she saw him stop in front of Fannie Mae Byler, smiling and chatting.

It was like she was invisible, she thought miserably. Her shoulders slumped as she turned back to Sarah. "Did you say something?"

"He's nothing but a big flirt," Sarah told her sympathetically.

Ruby sighed. She knew that. The only time he'd ever paid attention to her was when he'd sat behind her in Schul when they were ten and he'd pulled on her braids.

"Here, help me pass out the hymnals," Sarah said, so Ruby walked over to where the others were gathering and began handing them out.

Then she took her place in the group and opened the hymnal to the song Sarah chose. She lifted her voice in song and felt joy surge through her as she sang the old, sacred hymns. Singing always lifted her spirits.

When Sarah called for a break, Ruby turned to Wayne Lapp, who was standing next to her. She had to look up quite a ways. Had he grown since the last time she'd seen him? She thought people stopped growing after they were teens.

"You have such a nice baritone, Wayne. I always enjoy hearing you sing."

"Danki," he said, his gaze already on the refreshment table.

"Try the brownies," she murmured as he left her.

First she was ignored for another Maedel, and then she came in second to the refreshments.

Feeling invisible, she joined Sarah at the table and helped pour lemonade and iced tea. There wasn't much time for chatting as they worked, but Ruby felt less enthusiasm for it as she watched couples forming while the others enjoyed the snacks and drinks.

It felt like Noah's Ark, she thought wryly. This was one of the few times the young Amish men and women got to mingle after long days of working and doing chores. So they made the most of it. After the break and more singing, those couples headed for their buggies to spend the drive home together, talking and laughing.

Ruby drove home alone, telling herself alone didn't mean lonely. But she felt it.

Ruby knew something was wrong the minute she walked into the house after work the next day.

The picnic basket she'd taken to her Aenti's house the evening before sat on the kitchen table, and her Dat was patting her Mudder's shoulder as she cried.

She dropped her purse on the bench beside the door and rushed to her Mudder's side. "Mamm, what's wrong?"

"Leah called and wants to talk to us."

"Why are you upset?"

"She was supposed to get her test results back this afternoon," Miriam said as she wiped her eyes.

"I know you're upset," her Dat said. "But, Miriam, you need to wait to hear what Leah was told. Don't jump to conclusions."

"But, Ben, if it's not bad news, why didn't she just say so over the phone?" Miriam asked him, her voice breaking.

"I don't know," he crooned, rubbing his big hand across her slender shoulders. "But we're not helpless. We can pray for Leah, the three of us, right now. And whatever it is, we'll sit down with her and figure out how we can help her."

"I was just there this morning, and she didn't say anything," Ruby said, confused.

"She must have heard something after you left for your job."

Ruby sat down in the chair next to her Mudder and reached for her hand. "We'll take care of her, Mamm. She won't go through whatever it is alone."

Miriam nodded and wiped her nose with her handkerchief. She glanced at the clock on the wall. "I better get supper started."

"Let me." Ruby stood. "Tell me what you were planning."

Her Mudder opened her mouth, but Ben shook his head. "Let Ruby cook, and let's go for a walk, the two of us, Miriam. Get some fresh air. It'll do you some *gut*."

She sighed. "I look a wreck."

He kissed the top of her head and then drew her to her feet. "You do not. *Komm*."

Miriam started out of the room with him and then stopped. "There's leftover baked chicken from yesterday," she told Ruby. "I was going to make a chicken, broccoli, and rice casserole out of it."

"I can do that. Have a nice walk."

Ruby watched them leave the room and thought, *Two by two.* They had each other, but Leah would be fighting her health battle alone. Her *Mann*, Eli Stoltzfus, had died years ago, leaving her a Wittfraa.

She wondered if Leah felt lonely right now and decided that as soon as supper was over, she would take a walk of her own and visit her.

Leah had always been her favorite Aenti. They'd had a special bond for years. Ruby decided Leah wasn't going to face this by herself if she had anything to say about it.

Daniel walked his fields and nodded with satisfaction as he viewed the tender green shoots of corn emerging from the rich brown earth and reaching up for the warmth of the spring sun.

His Dat had once said farming was a lot like being an Eldre. Both started with something small and vulnerable, and you watched over them and nurtured them and worked hard to trust

God that both crop and Kinna grew strong and healthy and weathered the storms of life.

He'd hoped he'd have a partner to share the joys and the challenges of raising Kinna, but that was evidently not part of His plan for him. It was nearing two years since Sadie had died, and he still wasn't ready to remarry.

He remembered how Leah had brought up the subject yesterday evening and he'd reminded her that Isaac had done so as well. The members of his community were fervent believers in marriage and encouraged widows and widowers to remarry— especially if they were young.

Well, just as you couldn't harvest a crop before its time, you couldn't nudge a man into remarrying before he was ready.

But if the not-so-subtle persuasion of adults wasn't working, the things your Kinna said tugged on the heartstrings . . . and the guilt.

Last night, he'd burned one of the grilled cheese sandwiches he'd made for supper, and Mary had shaken her head sadly at it on the plate and said Mudders didn't burn food. And when he'd checked on Samuel before he went to bed, he found him clutching the stuffed bunny that had been his Mudder's last Christmas gift to him.

Did other *Wittmenner* feel such sadness and guilt when they didn't marry quickly after they lost their Fraa? he wondered.

Maybe the next time he saw Lester Zook, he should get up the courage to ask him instead of staying with the usual topics of conversation like the weather and how his crops were doing and who needed help in the church community. Schur, things like that were important—the weather was especially important to a farmer, after all. But maybe sharing a deeper conversation would relieve some of the inner struggles Daniel felt as a single Eldre. He had no idea how he'd start such a conversation. Most of the men he knew didn't talk about feelings and such. But he wasn't the only one who felt them, was he?

He hoped not.

Hunger and thirst drove him inside at noon. He slapped together a ham and cheese sandwich and ate it with two glasses of iced tea. It was hours until suppertime, but he'd learned if he wanted to serve it to hungry Kinna on time, he had to think ahead. He didn't know how to cook a lot of different dishes, and the ones he prepared the most often were those he knew Mary and Samuel would eat without a fuss. He still had a few jars of spaghetti sauce his Mudder had canned last harvest and a pound of hamburger in the refrigerator. They ate a lot of hamburger. It was something that was fast and easy to cook, and the kids liked it.

Daniel felt he was a *gut* farmer, but he could use some lessons in cooking. It wasn't that he had never cooked when Sadie was alive. It was just that she was so much better at it that he'd sort of been lazy about doing much cooking. Now he was paying the price.

He went out and worked in the fields for a couple more hours. Glancing over at Leah's, he saw that Gideon was walking out to check on the rows of corn. He hadn't talked to the older man in a few days, so he headed over for their usual update.

Gideon raised a hand in welcome when he saw Daniel approaching. He was in his forties and had worked with Eli on the farm and continued after Eli died. Gideon and Daniel compared notes on how much growth Leah's corn was showing and commented on the all-important predictions for the weather for the coming week.

Leah was lucky to have such a *gut* caretaker as Gideon. It meant that she could stay in the home she'd lived in with Eli for decades and not have to sell it and move. Daniel had done as much as he could to help, as he'd promised Eli he would before he died.

"I'm heading into town for some supplies," Gideon said. "Need anything?"

Daniel shook his head. "I'm fine, but Danki."

Gideon headed for the barn, and Daniel walked out of the fields toward the house. He didn't usually visit Leah this time of day, but something drew him. As he approached the steps leading up to the back porch, Leah came to the door and opened it. She stood there, silent, unsmiling.

"Come in," she said quietly. "I heard from the doctor's office."

He stopped midstride when he saw the look in her eyes. And then he climbed the stairs slowly, dreading the news.

She took a seat at the table, so he did as well.

"It's leukemia."

"He's schur? Maybe you should get a second opinion."

She patted his hand, and he noticed how thin and frail her hand was. He could see the blue veins under the pale skin. "He had the tests run twice."

"So what's he going to do? There's a treatment, right? Wasn't David Miller's youngest diagnosed with leukemia when he was just a boy? And he had chemo, and he's fine now."

She nodded. "I'll be starting chemo very soon. And there's radiation. Even something called a stem-cell transplant as a last resort." She squeezed his hand. "But I'm going to be fine."

Stem. That made him think of the tender shoots of corn in her fields. A stem was a living thing, right? It had to be a *gut* thing.

"What can I do?" he asked.

"You've been doing it, dear *Bu*, helping Gideon with the farm so that I can stay here like Eli wanted." She took a deep breath, then let it out. "I'm not ready to join Eli yet. I'm determined to beat this."

There was a commotion at the kitchen door—a babble of childish voices, knocks on the wood, and a hissed argument. "Daedi said we should!" he heard Mary say self-importantly.

Then the door opened, and his Kinna tumbled into the room.

"*Ach*, I see my well-behaved Kinna found me," he told Leah.

"You always say that if you're not home when we come from school, we're supposed to walk over here and see Leah," Mary told him.

Leah held open her arms. "And so you should. May I have a hug?"

Mary rushed into her arms, closely followed by Samuel.

Daniel felt a pang at the sight of the three hugging but made schur he was under control when Leah released them.

"How about a snack?" she asked them.

"Leah, you don't have to—"

"Shush, Daniel. We're all going to have cookies and milk. I baked some chocolate chip cookies this morning."

"She told Daedi to shush!" Samuel said, giggling.

Leah pulled a fat cookie from the jar and stuck it in Daniel's mouth. "I did!" she said with a chuckle. "Want some milk with that, Daniel?"

CHAPTER THREE

Ruby studied her Mudder's tense expression as she drove the *Familye* buggy over to Leah's house.

"Mamm, I'm schur Leah is going to be allrecht."

Her Mudder shook her head. "I'm worried. She didn't sound right."

Ruby didn't want to argue with her. It seemed to her that her Mudder would know her Schweschder better than she would. "Try not to worry. We'll help her with whatever she has to tell us."

Miriam looked over and smiled. "We will." She pulled into Leah's driveway, but before she could get out, Ruby stopped her.

"Mamm, let's pray again before we go in."

"That's a *gut* idea." She sighed. "Danki for reminding me."

They sat in the buggy and held hands and prayed before they got out.

When they walked into Leah's kitchen, Ruby was surprised to see Daniel sitting at the table, drinking a cup of coffee.

He stood immediately. "Hello, Miriam, Ruby." He turned to Leah. "I'll see you tomorrow."

"You don't have to go," Leah said.

"You need to talk to your Familye," he said gently.

"Daniel, you're Familye," Leah said.

He smiled. "And you're mine. But you need time with Miriam and Ruby. I'm next door if you need me." He nodded at them and left.

"It's bad news," Miriam said, then burst into tears.

"Now, now, everything's going to be allrecht," Leah told her and gathered her into her arms for a long moment. "Komm, Miriam, sit." She urged Miriam into a chair and laid a comforting hand on her shoulder.

Ruby felt just as overwhelmed with emotion at Leah's demeanor, but her Aenti didn't need two overemotional women on her hands. She held out her arms, and Leah went into them. Ruby frowned when it seemed that Leah returned the hug with more intensity than usual, so she held her, wishing the woman didn't feel thinner, more frail than she had the last time she'd hugged her.

"Sit; tell us what's wrong," she said, and now she was the one who was guiding someone into a chair, laying a hand on her shoulder for comfort.

Leah did as Ruby asked and took a deep breath. "Doctor said the tests show I have leukemia—a kind of blood cancer."

Miriam cried harder. Ruby reached for the box of tissues she spotted on a counter and handed it to her.

"I was afraid you'd take it this way," Leah said and sighed. "I wasn't going to tell you."

"Why would you do that?" Miriam cried, then pulled a couple of tissues from the box and mopped at her eyes. "Why would you hide being ill from us?"

"Because I knew it would upset you like this. And it can be treated."

"Don't make it sound like you just take a couple of pills," Miriam told her with a touch of anger in her voice. "I remember when one of David Miller's Sohns had it; he got sick from the chemotherapy."

"That was years ago," Leah reminded her. "Not everyone has the same reaction. And I'm schur treatment has improved since then."

"When does the doctor want you to start treatment?" Ruby asked her.

"Next week."

Ruby stood. "I'm going to fix us some tea." She filled the kettle with water, set it on the stove, then turned to her Aenti. "Have you eaten today?"

"I had a sandwich for lunch," Leah said with a shrug. "I'm not really hungerich."

"You need to eat to keep up your strength," Ruby told her, then walked over to look in the refrigerator. Just as she suspected, there was a plate with half of an egg-salad sandwich wrapped in cling film sitting on the top shelf. Her Aenti hadn't eaten a sandwich at lunch—she'd eaten half of one.

"A body can't eat like a bird and fight an illness," she muttered. She spotted a clear plastic container of split-pea soup, found a pan, and poured the soup into it to warm on the stove. While she waited for it, she set cups of hot water on the table with the box of her Aenti's favorite tea bags, then unwrapped the half sandwich and placed the plate before Leah.

"My practical Ruby," she said with a smile.

Ruby ladled the soup into a bowl and set it next to Leah's plate. "What else can I get you?"

"Nothing, Danki. Please sit and drink your tea."

Ruby did as she was asked and was relieved to see that her Mudder was regaining her composure. The two Schweschders were so different. Leah was calm, even with such upsetting news. Ruby had seen that her Mudder often reacted very emotionally to things at first but then worked, as she did now, to regain her composure. Ruby thought she was more like her Aenti than her Mudder. She could usually cope with things without getting emotional first and deal with her feelings later.

And she knew she'd be doing that later tonight, after she returned home. Now, right now, she wanted to support Leah however she could.

Miriam blew her nose and then got to her feet. "I'm going to go wash my face," she said in a shaky voice. As she passed Leah, she bent to hug her. Then tears welled up in her eyes again, and she rushed out of the room.

"I still think it might have been best if I could have kept the news from your Mudder," Leah said quietly.

"I don't agree. That wouldn't be fair to you. Even if treatment goes as well as we hope, there may be times you need help, and you should get that. Mamm will cope. You'll see."

She rose and refilled their cups. "So, was Daniel here when you got the news?" she asked as she sipped her tea.

"He came over to talk with Gideon like he usually does each day. He helps Gideon sometimes," Leah told her. "He asked me yesterday if I'd heard from the doctor, so today when I saw him, I told him the news."

"He sounds like he's been a friend, not just a neighbor. He was years ahead of me in Schul and had his eye on Sadie even back then." She frowned. "It is so sad that he and their Kinna lost her."

Leah nodded, and then she looked thoughtful. "Ruby, would you be willing to help me for a few weeks? Go with me to treatments, help me out around the house and such?"

The request was so unexpected, Ruby just stared at her for a moment. Leah never, ever asked for help. Even when her Mann had died, she hadn't asked anyone for help. Ruby felt a chill come over her. Was Leah more frightened, feeling worse than she was letting on?

"Of course," she said quickly. "You didn't need to ask. I'll get my things together and come over tomorrow."

Daniel walked his fields the next day, checking the growth of his crops, feeling a too-familiar cold ball of fear in his stomach.

He hadn't wanted Leah to know he was afraid for her. But he was. Both of them knew too much about loss. She'd lost her Mann several years before he'd received the devastating news that his Fraa had been killed in a traffic accident. He didn't know if he'd have gotten through the pain, the loneliness without her quiet wisdom and support.

Leah had never once said she knew what he was feeling, the way some well-meaning friends and neighbors had. Instead, she'd sat and listened to him over endless cups of coffee and tea, cooked meals, and taken the Kinna and helped them with their grief when he felt like he was just putting one foot in front of the other and failing them.

She was a friend and a Grossmudder figure—and his guide out of the darkness of loss.

She had to survive this. She'd become much too important to him and his Kinna.

And when he told her one day what she had come to mean to him and the Kinna, she'd explained how they, in turn, had helped to heal her grieving heart.

He threw himself into his chores, and his spirits lifted when he heard the commotion that heralded his Kinna coming home from school.

Samuel ran up to him in the barn, bursting to tell him about his day at Schul. "Daed, it was so funny! John ate his lunch and then barfed!"

"Barfed?" Daniel winced at the word and looked at Mary.

She rolled her eyes. "Why do *Buwe* think that's funny? It was gross, and our teacher had to clean it up."

"And how was your day?" he asked as they walked into the house. He washed his hands and listened to her tell him about the reaction Teacher Lovina had to her essay.

The Kinna settled at the kitchen table with an after-Schul snack while he enjoyed the break with a mug of coffee.

"So what's for supper?" Samuel wanted to know after he polished off his apple and a pile of cheese cubes.

"You just had a snack," he reminded him.

"Well, we'll be hungerich soon."

"He will be," Mary said with another roll of her eyes.

Daniel tried to remember if his Schweschder had rolled her eyes as much at him when they were growing up. He didn't think so. They chattered—both of his Kinna loved to talk—and bickered, another favorite activity. He listened and intervened occasionally, but he'd learned not to try to settle arguments too often. They'd be friends two seconds after the most heated of disagreements, whether about an event that had happened at Schul or whose turn it was to set the table.

Sometimes he wondered if same-sex siblings got along any better than those of opposite sexes. Well, he'd have to ask one of his friends who had Kinna. He doubted he was going to get remarried anytime soon and find out for himself.

He finished his coffee and relieved Samuel's worries about what they'd have for supper by setting out the ingredients for spaghetti before they gathered supplies to wash windows.

He'd had to rely on Leah to know how to do some of these simple household chores. She'd teased him about being a *Hausfraa* when he'd asked for cleaning tips and recipes for simple meals and then supplied him with binders for both a week later.

Now, as he and the Kinna worked on the windows, he glanced over at her house and wondered what he could do to give her support as she moved into a new phase of her life, fighting her illness.

"Daedi?"

"Hmm?" He glanced down at Mary and found her frowning up at him.

"What's wrong? You're frowning."

He gave her a big, goofy grin. "Don't know what you're talking about."

She giggled. "Silly Daedi."

Daniel told himself he had to be careful. He knew he'd gone through a dark period after he'd lost Sadie, and Leah had sat him down and made him aware that he needed to pull himself together for the sake of his Kinna. They were grieving too—Mary more than Samuel because she was older and remembered her Mudder more. Leah had been the best of friends and had said the tough words when they were needed.

"I think we should see if Leah's windows need to be washed after Schul tomorrow," he said.

Samuel nodded. "We can do that. Bet she'd give us some cookies. She always has cookies."

Mary rolled her eyes. "We will do them without asking for cookies."

"We will," Daniel said firmly.

A few minutes later, Leah came out onto her porch, looked over, and waved. She walked over and said hello.

"Fine job," she told them. "The windows are sparkling."

"We'll come do yours next," Mary offered before Daniel could speak up.

Leah smiled and patted her head. "Danki, *Lieb*." She looked at Daniel. "The Kinner has a *gut* heart."

"I do too!" Samuel cried.

Leah chuckled and ruffled his hair. "*Ya*, you do." She glanced up at Daniel, and her smile faded. "All of you do."

A buggy pulled up in front of the house, and Ben, Ruby's Dat, waved to them. Ruby emerged from the vehicle and walked up to join them on the porch as he drove away. She carried a small suitcase, which she set down beside her as she greeted everyone.

"Ruby has come to live with me for a while," Leah told them.

"Why?" Samuel wanted to know.

Leah smiled. "Because she has a *gut* heart and wants to help me."

"We do too," he told Ruby.

"I'm schur you do," she said with a shy smile.

"Well, Ruby, let's go get you settled," Leah said briskly.

Daniel watched as Ruby had to move quickly to pick up her suitcase before Leah did, then hurried to keep up with her as they walked to the neighboring house.

CHAPTER FOUR

"Stop worrying."

Ruby stared at her Aenti as they drove to town. "I'm beginning to wonder why you asked me to move in with you. I don't think you need my help."

"Of course I do. I just want to go into town and do a little shopping."

"But you really should rest."

"I did fine with the first treatment. Now are you going to relax and enjoy going into town or not?"

Ruby sighed. "Ya."

"We both deserve a little treat after the last week, don't you think? You gave up a lot to come live with me, and you've worked hard to clean my house this week."

"I didn't give up anything, Leah. My job wasn't working out. Just like other jobs I've tried." She stared out at the passing scenery, feeling a little depressed.

"That's because you're not doing your true calling. You're not using your talents."

"I have no talents."

"That's not true. You just haven't taken time to find what you should be doing."

Ruby looked over at her. "A job is to make money."

"It doesn't have to be only that. You have a wonderful sense of color when you choose fabrics for a quilt. You should be doing more of them."

"Takes a long time to make a quilt. You know that. I wanted to help Mamm and Daed after they had some extra bills last year, so that's why I took the job in town."

"And now it's time for you to do something for yourself," Leah told her as they approached town and traffic increased. "I want you to pick out some fabrics for a quilt. And a dress or two." She caught Ruby's eye. "Some colorful fabrics. What you've been wearing is drab. And getting worn out."

Ruby winced. Leah never believed in mincing words.

Leah parked in the lot behind the quilt shop. "I know I'm being blunt. But I've learned that time isn't to be wasted, Lieb. Now, let's go spend some time in one of my favorite places."

"That would be the art supply store, not the quilt shop," she pointed out.

She chuckled. "Now you're showing some spunk. Ya, first the quilt shop, then, ya, the art supply store."

They spent two hours in the quilt shop and far too many dollars. Leah insisted on Ruby choosing fabrics to make two dresses and a quilt. And she insisted that Ruby choose brighter colors than she was used to wearing.

Ruby loved the colors and patterns in the fabrics for the quilts, but she wasn't schur she was entirely comfortable with the rose pink and periwinkle blue for dresses.

But she decided to let Leah have her way. She was just so grateful that her Aenti was feeling better than she'd hoped after her first treatment.

The visit to the art supply store was shorter. Leah knew exactly what supplies she needed and didn't waste time selecting them.

And then she admitted her energy was flagging, and they climbed into the buggy to head back. Leah let Ruby take the driver's seat and slept all the way home. When Leah's horse turned down the drive, Leah woke. "Guess I fell asleep for a few minutes there," she said, blinking sleepily.

Ruby laughed. "You slept all the way from town." She got out of the buggy and began unhitching it.

Leah gathered the shopping bags before climbing out. "I'll make us some lunch."

"You go in and sit down," Ruby called after her. "I'll be in and fix lunch in a minute." She led Willow, Leah's horse, into the barn. "Woman wears me out," she told the horse as she put her in a stall and made schur she had water.

When she walked into the kitchen, she saw that Leah hadn't listened to her. The makings for sandwiches were already on the table, and her Aenti was pouring glasses of lemonade.

Ruby quickly washed her hands and sat at the table, unable to take her eyes off her Aenti. Leah scooped tuna salad from a container and made herself a sandwich, then passed the container to Ruby.

They ate and talked about their shopping trip. When they'd finished, Ruby insisted on clearing the table. Ruby then began looking through the bags from the quilt shop, and Leah watched as Ruby spread the rose-colored fabric out and pinned on the pattern pieces.

"How long has it been since you had a new dress?" Leah asked as Ruby cut out the pieces.

Ruby shrugged. "I'm not that interested in clothes."

"Ha! What Maedel isn't interested in clothes?"

"Well, Mamm and Daed needed help, and I didn't mind giving them my paycheck. Hopefully, things will be better this year with the farm."

She wondered how Leah had done last year with the farm but didn't know how to ask without seeming nosy. She knew Gideon and Daniel and other men from the community had helped her with it so that she hadn't had to sell it after her Mann died. But that's all she knew.

After stacking the cut pieces, Ruby set them aside and started on the other length of fabric. She found herself getting excited about having something new to wear in spite of what she'd said to Leah. She wasn't vain. She really didn't mind not having anything new for a long time. But it had bothered her when her dresses had started looking faded and worn.

There was a knock on the door, and Daniel poked his head in. "You're back," he said, looking at Leah as he stepped into the room.

She nodded. "We went into town for a while."

"So you're feeling allrecht?"

"Just fine. Stop worrying. You and Ruby are a pair of worrywarts."

Samuel came from behind his Dat's legs and stared at Leah. "What's a worrywart?"

Leah chuckled. "Are you home from Schul already?"

He nodded vigorously. "What's a worrywart?"

"Why don't you go get my basket of art supplies from the bench by the door there, and I'll show you?" Leah invited. "Let's go sit on the porch so that Ruby can finish cutting out her dress."

After they left, Daniel turned to Ruby. "Do you think you should have taken Leah into town in her condition?" he asked her bluntly.

Surprised, she stared at him. "She wanted to go."

"You couldn't talk her out of it?"

"You know Leah," she told him. "She can't be talked out of anything when she wants to do it." Frowning, she placed the pieces she'd cut out on top of the new fabric. "And I tried."

She debated telling him Leah had slept all the way home and decided he'd just say that showed the trip had been too much for her Aenti.

"Daedi, are we going to wash windows for Leah?" Mary asked from the doorway.

"Schur," he said. "I'll be right there."

"What are you doing?" Mary asked Ruby.

"Cutting out a new dress." Ruby avoided looking at the Kinner's Dat.

"I like new dresses," Mary confided, moving closer. "Leah made me one for my birthday. It's pretty."

Ruby smiled. She was such a sweet Kinner. "I bet it is. What color is it?"

"Blue. My favorite color." She touched the rose-pink fabric. "I really like this color too."

"Leah chose it."

"Komm, Mary, let's get started on the windows," Daniel said abruptly.

Ruby frowned as she watched him shepherd his daughter out of the room and shut the door with a snap.

What was his problem?

Daniel stared down at the sketch Leah had made. "What is that?"

Samuel giggled. "It's a worrywart, Daedi!"

The animal she'd drawn looked like a porcupine, and he wore a great big grin. As Daniel watched, Leah drew a straw hat on the animal's head, then wrote "Daniel" beneath the animal's feet.

Samuel nearly fell off his chair laughing. Mary walked over to see what was going on, and she burst into giggles as well.

"Very funny." He frowned at Leah. "Really, do you think it was a *gut* idea to go gallivanting off to town to shop so soon after your treatment?"

"I'm fine, as you can see." She eyed the plastic bucket of window-washing supplies he carried. "Danki for wanting to wash my windows, Daniel, but Ruby and I could do it."

He thought Ruby seemed more interested in sewing herself a dress after their shopping jaunt but decided not to say so. Something about the glint in Leah's eyes warned him to keep his opinion to himself.

"Since we're back here, we might as well start on these windows," he said. "Come on, Samuel, you do this window, and Mary will do that one."

He gave them the supplies and started on a third window. "So when do you go for your next treatment?"

She glanced at the Kinna, then pointedly at him. "I think I'll go get something for us to drink," she said and headed for the door.

Allrecht, so maybe she didn't want them to know about what she was going through. He'd talk to her about it when they weren't around.

When Leah emerged, she was with Ruby, who was carrying a tray with a pitcher of lemonade and glasses.

Well, at least Ruby had left her sewing project and carried the tray out for her Aenti. The Kinna ran over when she set the tray on a table, each happily accepting a glass of lemonade and a sugar cookie with words of thanks.

"Lemonade, Daniel?" Ruby asked, offering him a glass.

He took it and a sugar cookie as well. It was a stupid man who didn't take a cookie baked by Leah when he had the chance. "Danki."

"I made both," she told him, looking at him directly. "In case you're worried I'm not helping Leah."

Before he could say anything, she'd turned and walked away.

He stuck the cookie in his mouth, wondering if there was room with his big foot in there. With a sigh, he turned his attention back to his Kinna. Schur enough, Samuel was tucking a cookie into his mouth.

"Samuel!"

He jumped. "What?" Crumbs flew.

"Don't put the whole cookie in your mouth at once! You'll choke."

"Worrywart," Samuel told him with a chuckle after he chewed and swallowed.

"You looked like a chipmunk," Mary told him with the disdain only an older Schweschder could show.

"I did not!"

Daniel told them to stop their bickering and get back to work, then turned to find Leah and Ruby having a quiet tug-of-war with the tray Ruby had brought the drinks out on.

"Well, I'm not going to sit here and not do anything," Leah said with a stubborn tilt to her chin.

"You sit right there. I have something you can do," Ruby said.

Leah let go of the tray. She sat there drumming her fingers on the arm of the chair.

Ruby looked pointedly at the basket of art supplies, and after a moment, Leah picked up her sketch pad again.

"I'll be inside," Ruby told her. "Yell if you need anything."

"Smart aleck," Leah muttered, but Daniel saw her lips twitch with a grin. Then she looked at him. "Did you say something?"

"Not a word," he said, tucking his tongue firmly in his cheek.

He noted that Samuel and Mary were nearly finished with their windows, and he hadn't gotten very far with his. He sprayed cleaner on the glass and used a rag to wipe away the grime. As he did, he saw Ruby looking at him from the other side as she stood at the kitchen sink, washing dishes.

She raised her eyebrows in question.

He shook his head and finished the window. "Come on—let's do the front windows."

When they walked into the kitchen, Ruby looked up. "Is Leah doing allrecht?"

"Ya, she's busy sketching."

The Kinna followed him through the house and out onto the front porch, where they immediately set about washing the windows there.

"Daedi, can we use the ladder to wash the windows up high like you do?" Samuel asked him.

"Absolutely not!" he said.

Samuel pouted as he went back to washing his window.

"Promise me you won't ever climb up on a ladder when I'm not around."

His Sohn just uttered a big sigh and nodded. "You're no fun," he muttered.

"I heard that."

Ruby walked out a few minutes later. "Time for more lemonade?"

"Ya!" Samuel cried. "And cookies?"

"Samuel."

He sobered at Daniel's stern tone. "I mean, yes, please, Ruby," he said and gave her an angelic smile.

"That's his Mr. Charm look," Daniel told her as he looked over from his window.

"Wonder who he got that from?" she murmured.

"I heard that."

"Daedi's got *gut* hearing," Mary told her as she walked over to Ruby. "He can always hear stuff, even when we whisper, and he says he has eyes in the back of his head too. I looked, though, and he doesn't."

"Telling all my secrets, are you?" he grumbled and made a grab for her.

She danced away, giggling.

"I'll get the lemonade," Ruby said.

"And the cookies!" Samuel called out.

"And the cookies."

Ruby went into the house, and Leah walked out a few minutes later, carrying her art basket.

"Almost done out there," Leah said, nodding with approval. "I have some hard workers. Danki, everyone."

"I asked Daedi if we could go on the ladder and clean the upstairs windows, but he said no," Samuel told her as she took a seat in a rocking chair.

"I appreciate your wanting to help that way, Samuel, but you need to wait a few years," she told him kindly. "Promise me you'll stay off ladders when your Dat isn't around."

He rolled his eyes. "I already promised Daedi."

"*Gut.*"

"Got lonely on the front porch all by myself," she said as she drew out her easel and soon was working away, her pencil flying on a fresh page of the sketch pad.

Ruby came out with a tray and set it on the table near Leah. Daniel watched his Kinna descend on it like a pack of hungry, thirsty wolves.

"One cookie," he said quickly, ignoring their moans.

They took glasses of lemonade from Ruby, chose a cookie, and made him proud when they thanked her without being told to.

Then they drifted over to see what Leah was sketching. That's when the giggles started.

"You have to see this," Mary said, covering her mouth to stop the giggles. But they sneaked out around her fingers. Samuel was laughing too.

Ruby wandered over to look at what Leah was working on. "Hey! That's not funny!"

Daniel came close and studied the drawing. Leah had sketched another porcupine-looking animal but had put a Kapp and an apron on this one and written "Ruby, the Worrywart" at the bottom.

He chuckled. "Now *that's* funny!"

Leah held up the sketch she'd made of him. "You didn't think this one was funny a little while ago."

"You made a pair of worrywarts," Mary told her as she leaned against Leah's arm.

"I did, didn't I?" Leah said thoughtfully as she looked at Daniel. "I schur did."

CHAPTER FIVE

Ruby slipped on her new rose-pink dress and looked at her reflection in the mirror.

A smile spread slowly over her face. The color made her skin glow and her brown eyes sparkle. Was it the color or the fact that she had a new dress—the first she'd had in several years?

Then her smile faded. Was it wrong to be happy to have something new? It wasn't prideful, was it? Sometimes it just felt so *gut* to put something on that made you feel pretty and young. That wasn't wrong, was it?

"I knew that was the right color for you," Leah said with satisfaction as she came into the room. "It looks *wunderbaar* on you."

"I really like it. I haven't had a dress this color in years."

Leah nodded. "I can't wait to see how the blue looks on you."

Ruby turned and threw her arms around her Aenti. "Danki for the fabric. I wish you'd let me pay for it."

"Nonsense. You're going to be helping me. Now, I need you to do something for me. Can you take this over to Daniel?" She held out a piece of paper. "He said he was going into town and asked if he could pick up anything for me."

"Schur. Just let me change and—"

"You need to take it now. He's leaving in a few minutes."

"Oh. Allrecht." She took the slip of paper.

"He'll be out in the barn," Leah told her.

"I'll be right back."

"You could go with him if you want to."

Ruby shook her head. "I want to start sewing the blue dress. Or maybe look through some of your quilt books. Then I thought I'd start supper."

"Allrecht. Just thought you might like to go to town."

"I just went to town."

"With me. It'd be a lot more interesting with Daniel than with your old Aenti."

"I had fun with you, and don't be talking like you're old. Now let me get this to Daniel before he leaves."

She hurried off on her errand and soon found Daniel hitching a horse to his buggy. "I brought Leah's list. She said you were picking up some things for her in town."

He stared at her. "Going somewhere?"

"Nee. Why do you ask?"

"You seem dressed up."

Ruby let herself blush under his study. "Nee." She shrugged. "Just a new dress I finished sewing—Leah wanted to see it on me. I'll tell Leah I passed on her message."

She walked away, feeling surprised at his noticing. Whenever the two of them had been around each other, he'd paid her little to no attention.

She glanced back, and their gazes locked. Quickly, she looked away and hurried toward her Aenti's house.

Leah looked up in surprise when Ruby walked into the kitchen. "I thought you might have changed your mind and gone with Daniel."

She shook her head. "I really want to stay here and do some sewing and look at quilt books. I'm going to change."

When she came back downstairs in one of her everyday dresses, Leah sat at the kitchen table with a stack of books in front of her.

"You could make a chicken casserole with the leftovers in the refrigerator, and then we could look over the books while it bakes," Leah suggested.

"Sounds like a *gut* idea." Ruby gathered ingredients and set about assembling the casserole while they chatted. After it was in the oven, she made them cups of tea and joined her Aenti at the table.

"It's been a while since I sewed a quilt," Ruby said as she leafed through a book of Amish quilt patterns. "I haven't had much time, working and helping Mamm around the house."

"Which is your favorite pattern of all the ones you've worked with?"

"I like the wedding ring pattern, and it's popular."

"The one you donated to the Haiti auction sold for a high price," Leah said. "I remember Lillian at the quilt shop in town said she'd take any quilt you made for sale in her shop."

"She was very kind to say so."

"She wasn't being kind. She's a businesswoman. She wouldn't take work that was less than excellent. Remember, she has a reputation to uphold."

Ruby took note of Leah's tone and felt chastened.

Leah patted her hand. "My dear, you need to value yourself more. God gives us all some talent, and it honors Him to use it."

Ruby glanced at the clever little sketches of vegetables that Leah had done and framed that hung on the walls of her sunny-yellow kitchen. She'd been sketching for as long as Ruby could remember.

"I know it's not easy at first, but it's the doing that will build your self-confidence," she said gently. "It's a little like learning to walk. At first, we fall down a lot. But then it gets easier, until we're walking and we don't even think about those first tough steps."

"I suppose." Ruby turned the pages of the book in front of her. "I know sunshine and shadow quilts are always popular, but I don't want to work on one of those right now."

"Allrecht. Then let's find a pattern you do want to work on."

Ruby pored over the books and found her interest growing. "I remember going to the quilting circle with you and Mamm. I was about five, and I crawled under the quilt frame." She'd lain there, watching the needles flashing in and out of the fabric. The motion of the needles was rhythmic and hypnotic, and she'd fallen asleep there on the floor.

"You scared us," Leah told her. "We thought you'd wandered off, and we called you and called you. Then you came crawling out from under the quilt frame."

"You taught me how to thread a needle and gave me my first quilt square to work on. I didn't take any more naps under the quilt frame after that. I loved sitting and learning to sew and quilt."

Leah chuckled and rose to turn off the oven timer. "How time flies. It doesn't seem possible you're twenty-two." She used potholders to take the casserole out of the oven and set it on the stove.

"I think I want to make a wedding ring quilt," Ruby said. "Lillian would find a buyer quickly with so many *Englischers* getting married in summer."

When she went to bed that night, visions of quilts danced in her head.

Daniel was keeping a sharp eye on Mary as she sat at the kitchen table and chopped vegetables for a salad.

He wasn't worried she'd hurt herself. Leah had given him great advice when Mary started asking him to teach her how to cook. Leah had told him to give Mary a plastic knife, and she was busily using it, her tongue caught between her teeth, as she sliced a big tomato and put the slices on top of the greens.

Daniel hoped that Samuel, sitting at the table coloring, would develop some interest in cooking or, at the very least, eating the contents of the colander of fresh vegetables the three of them had picked from the kitchen garden.

But when he offered his Sohn a carrot stick and a little bowl of ranch dressing to dip it in, Samuel just wrinkled his nose and shook his head.

A few minutes later, Daniel caught Samuel peeling the wrapper off an orange crayon. He watched, wondering what the Bu was going to do, and then saw him hide it in the bowl of carrot sticks and nudge it closer to Mary. Frowning, Daniel fished out the crayon and handed it back to Samuel with a stern warning that it was to color with, not something to try to get his Schweschder to eat.

Shaking his head, Daniel put the bowl of salad in the refrigerator to chill. As he shut the door, he tried not to look at Leah's drawing of a worrywart that Mary had attached to it with magnets.

He couldn't help remembering how Leah had sketched two worrywarts—one that was supposed to be him and one that was supposed to be Ruby.

"Daed? What are we going to make for supper?"

"We have some hamburger meat, and we have hot dogs," he said as he opened the refrigerator again and peered inside.

"We could make beanie wienies with the hot dogs," she said. "Why do we call them wieners *and* hot dogs?"

"I have no idea."

She got down from her chair and went to get the wooden recipe box from the kitchen counter. After she climbed back into her chair, she leafed through the box, found a card, and pulled it out with a grin.

"For beanie wienies, it says we need a package of wieners, a big can of baked beans, and some bacon," she read slowly and carefully. "And brown sugar and ketchup." She looked up at him. "I want to make that. Me and Samuel like it a lot."

"Samuel and I," he corrected.

"Ya, I know you like it." She giggled when he frowned. "I know, it's *Samuel and I*, not *me and Samuel*." She hopped down. "I can get all the stuff, and we can make it, right?"

"I want beanie wienies," Samuel affirmed as he looked up from his coloring.

Daniel figured that was because it didn't have any "vegedabbles."

"We'll have that, but everyone has to eat some salad."

Samuel rolled his eyes and sighed.

"What's it mean to preheat?" Mary asked as she squinted at the card.

Daniel looked at her with alarm. "Mary, are you having trouble reading the card?" He hoped she didn't need glasses.

She used her thumb to rub at the card. "It has something spilled on it. What's 'preheat'?"

"It means to turn the oven on so that it gets nice and hot before we need to use it."

"Oh. Allrecht." She told him the temperature to set the oven on. "I'd do it, but you told us not to touch anything on the stove."

"That's right." Feeling proud of her, he kissed the top of her head and poured himself a cup of coffee.

Mary busied herself assembling the casserole, with Daniel's help. He opened the big can of pork and beans she got from the pantry, and she dumped it into the dish and added the proper amount of brown sugar and ketchup. Then, after she deemed she'd stirred it enough, she used the plastic knife to slice the wieners lengthwise and place them on top of the beans in just the pattern she wanted. The final touch was strips of bacon on top.

Daniel set the dish in the oven while Mary carefully washed her hands. "How many minutes should this bake, Mary?"

After she dried her hands, she walked over to sit at the table again and studied the card. "It says half an hour or until the bacon is browned and the casserole is bubbly." She replaced the card and flipped through the rest of them in the box.

"Daedi, you said we have hamburger. Mamm's got lots of recipes for hamburger."

Daniel nodded. "Your Mudder was very good at stretching a dollar."

"Why do you pull on a dollar?" she asked, looking confused.

He choked back a laugh. "It's an expression. It means being *gut* at making the money you have go a long way. You're good at making it go far."

When she still looked like she didn't understand, he searched for a better way to explain it. "She was careful with money and could make a small amount buy everything we needed. Hamburger doesn't cost much, and you can make a big meal out of it."

"Oh. Allrecht. And we like hamburger." She continued to look through the recipes. "We could make tacos and spaghetti and hamburger soup this week."

He thought that sounded like a lot of hamburger in one week, but he didn't want to dampen her enthusiasm. So he pulled a pad of paper and a pencil from a kitchen drawer and handed them to her. "Write out a menu, a list of what you want to help cook each day, and put it on the refrigerator. And make some nights something with some chicken and something not-hamburger."

"Macaroni and cheese!" Samuel piped up.

She nodded. "Daedi and I will make it one night if you tell us one vegetable you'll eat with us."

Daniel stared at her, impressed. She was acting like a little Mudder.

Samuel wrinkled his nose and frowned in concentration. "Green beans," he said with a big sigh.

Mary wrote that down. After she finished her list, she handed it to Daniel for approval.

He nodded. "We can do this." Even though he knew they had the ingredients for everything, he told her to look at the recipe cards, check the pantry, and make a list of what was needed for the next couple of nights.

By the time she was finished and posted the menu on the refrigerator, the casserole was done and ready to come out. He wouldn't let her near the stove for a few more years at least, so he took it out and set it on a trivet on the table, then turned off the oven.

He watched her close the recipe box and hug it to her chest as she carried it back to the counter where they kept it, then patted it.

"You like looking through the recipe box?" he asked her as he got out plates to set the table.

"It's a memory box," she told him seriously.

"A memory box?"

She nodded. "I remember all the delicious things Mamm made for us to eat."

"Like macaroni and cheese," Samuel said with a nod.

Daniel felt a funny little clutch in his chest as they talked. Sometimes he wondered how much they remembered about her. He talked about her occasionally and always answered any questions they had about her. Should he do that more? Maybe he needed to ask Leah for her advice about that.

His gaze went to the sketch on the refrigerator. He remembered what Mary had said after watching Leah finish a second sketch of what she called a worrywart.

"You made a pair of worrywarts," Mary had told her as she leaned against Leah's arm.

"I did, didn't I?" Leah had said, and she'd looked thoughtfully at Daniel. "I did."

He wondered if she had matchmaking on her mind.

Well, he didn't feel ready to think about remarrying. But as the three of them gathered at the big wooden table, he felt a twinge of guilt that maybe his Kinna wanted a Mudder—and not just for the delicious things she made for them to eat.

But marriages were forever in his community. He needed to make the right choice. Did God set aside more than one person for you? He'd seen some widowers remarry—but not all.

Besides, they were doing fine right now, weren't they? There was no rush.

CHAPTER SIX

"Wear one of your new dresses."

Ruby glanced over to see Leah standing in the doorway of her room. "To have supper with your neighbors?"

Leah nodded vigorously. "It's a special occasion."

"What would that be?"

"Mary invited us. She's learning to cook."

"Should we take some Pepto Bismol before we go?" Ruby asked as she slipped into her new periwinkle-blue dress. "I remember my first efforts."

Leah chuckled. "Be nice."

Ruby walked to the mirror over her dresser to pin on a fresh Kapp. "You know I won't say anything. She's so sweet. Both the Kinna are."

She didn't say they were nicer than Daniel. He was Leah's friend, so she decided he must have some redeeming qualities.

"I think I like that color on you even better than the rose," Leah told her.

"Me too." She sighed. It felt so *gut* to wear something new. So far, she'd only had the rose dress on for a little while, when she'd run next door to give Daniel Leah's list, and she'd just finished the blue one.

"Ready to go?"

Ruby hesitated. "Are you schur you feel up to it? You came home not feeling well after your treatment this morning."

"I was fine after a rest. And I'll be sitting down, eating."

She wanted to argue, but her Aenti had a mind of her own. And maybe she'd eat more than she usually did. "I hope I don't spill anything on this new dress."

Leah hugged her. "Don't be silly. It would wash right out. And we should enjoy things, not save them. We don't know how long we have here on Earth."

"True." But she wasn't going to wear her new dresses just anywhere. Who knew when she'd get new ones again?

They walked over to Daniel's house.

"You can tell it's spring," Ruby said, wrinkling her nose as the aroma of fertilizer drifted on the breeze from the freshly planted fields.

As they climbed the steps up to the back porch, Ruby happened to glance over and saw a pile of leaves stacked up like a nest and a great big frog sitting atop it.

After a brief knock on the door, Leah opened it and walked inside. Ruby followed, and her fears about the meal vanished when the scents hit her.

"Something smells delicious," Leah said, and Mary rushed over to hug her.

"I made a baked chicken," the girl told her.

"It's the second time this week," Samuel complained.

"I wanted to make schur it was going to be *gut*," she said, glaring at him. "You don't have to eat it if you don't like it."

"Ya, he does," Daniel corrected. "Hello, Leah, Ruby. We're glad you could come."

It had to be her imagination that his gaze lingered on her, Ruby decided as Daniel invited them to sit at the big kitchen table.

Daniel's farmhouse was in stark contrast to the one she'd grown up in. His was so much larger, newer, and better kept up. It wasn't showy, but the furniture, the plates, everything seemed so fine—not just better quality than that in her own home but even Leah's. Obviously, Daniel's farm was doing well. She was glad she had listened to Leah and worn something new; she thought she might have felt a little underdressed in one of the old ones that had become so worn-looking.

"Can we help with anything?" Leah asked, but Mary shook her head.

"You're our guests tonight," she said with an air of importance. "Daed let me do everything but put the chicken in the oven."

Ruby glanced at him, and her heart warmed at the look of pride on his face. She also noted that he watched his *Dochder* carefully, protectively, as she moved back to the stove to stir something in a pot. When she went to pick it up, he was out of his chair like he'd been shot out of a slingshot and made her stand aside as he poured the steaming green beans from the pot into the bowl.

He put that on the table and then got a roasting pan from the oven and transferred a plump, golden chicken from it to a platter. Then he relented and let her help carry one side of the ceramic platter and place it in the center of the table.

"Why, I've never seen a finer-looking baked chicken," Leah said, smiling at Mary. "Have you, Ruby?"

"Nee, it looks wunderbaar."

Samuel rolled his eyes but said nothing when his Dat looked at him.

A bowl of mashed potatoes with browned butter atop joined the bowl of green beans. Daniel sat and said the blessing, and then he carved the chicken while the bowls were passed around and everyone helped themselves.

"Delicious," Leah proclaimed as she tried a bite of chicken. "It's as *gut* as your Mudder's used to be."

"I used her recipe," Mary said earnestly.

"Familye recipes are the best," Ruby said. "This is delicious."

She tried not to be obvious in looking to see how much Leah was eating and was relieved to see that she had taken a *gut*-size slice of chicken and had a small mound of green beans on her plate.

"Daedi lets me plan the menus now. And I get to cook some of them. But he says he can't help me much with learning how to bake."

"I love to bake," Ruby said. "I could teach you."

Mary's eyes widened. "Could you?"

"Schur. If it's allrecht with your Dat."

"Please, Daedi. I want to learn how to make biscuits. And cinnamon rolls."

"I'm schur Ruby's busy," Daniel began.

"Nee, I'm schur I could find the time to teach you how to bake something. We could use your kitchen, couldn't we, Leah?"

"Absolutely. Especially if I get to taste test."

"I want to taste test," Samuel spoke up.

"We'll see," Daniel said.

Samuel frowned and pushed the green beans around on his plate.

Ruby's *Bruder*, who lived out of state now, had never shown an interest in the kitchen, except for eating, so she didn't know how to respond. Clearly, he felt left out. "What's your favorite treat, Samuel? Your favorite cookie or cake or pie?"

She got a shrug from him, and he got a stern look from his Dat.

"Samuel's favorite cookies are snickerdoodles," Daniel told her. "Leah bakes them for him sometimes."

"You could come over and bake them with me sometime," she told Samuel and won a small smile from him. "Then you can be the first taste tester when they come out of the oven."

He shot his Schweschder a gloating look.

"I like your dress," Mary said suddenly as she stared at Ruby.

"Why, Danki," she said. "I just made it."

"Leah made mine. It's almost the same color as yours."

"It is. It's very pretty on you."

Mary glowed and then stood. "We're having ice cream for dessert."

Daniel stood and looked at Samuel. "Komm—let's clear the table."

"I can help," Ruby offered, but Daniel shook his head firmly.

"Like Mary said, you and Leah are our guests tonight."

"I see someone put my sketch of your Dat on the refrigerator," Leah said as Mary got a half gallon of ice cream from the freezer.

"I did," Mary confided.

Ruby saw Daniel frown and glance at her, then away.

What was that about? she wondered. And then Mary's words as she handed over the sketch that day came back to her.

"You made a pair of worrywarts," Mary had told her as she leaned against Leah's arm.

Something made her glance at Mary then. Ruby found the girl watching her very intently, and Ruby wondered what she was thinking.

Daniel had been paying so much attention to Mary and making schur she stayed safe that he hadn't noticed that Samuel had disappeared.

One minute, he'd been clearing the table with Samuel's help, and the next, Samuel wasn't in the room.

Daniel had been a Bu himself. He remembered what he'd gotten up to when he had the chance, and he felt a bit of trepidation.

Leah rose just then, and Daniel looked at her. "Just going to get a glass of water," she said as she started toward the sink. "I can do that myself."

"Let me get that for you." He took the glass and filled it from the tap. "Would you like some ice in it?"

"Schur. Danki."

When he turned back, he saw Samuel was back in his seat and looking innocent.

Maybe he'd been paranoid to worry.

"Oh my!" Ruby cried, startling Daniel and causing him to bobble the glass.

A big frog had leaped from somewhere nearby and plopped down on the middle of her empty plate.

But instead of shrieking, she just laughed, plucked it up, and held it in her hands as she turned to Samuel.

"I believe this is yours. I saw him on the back porch when we came over."

His Sohn's expression of disappointment told Daniel everything he needed to know.

"Samuel!"

"What?" He held up his hands. "That's not my frog."

"Ya, it is," Mary said with disgust. She set down the container of ice cream, picked up Ruby's plate, and put it in the sink. "I saw you playing with it earlier today."

"How do you know it's the same frog?" he demanded, looking close to tears.

"Samuel! Take the frog and put it outside. Now."

He jumped to his feet, took the frog from Ruby, and rushed out the door with it. When he came back, Daniel sent him to the bathroom to wash his hands. Then, when he returned to the table, Daniel told him to apologize to Ruby.

"Sorry," he managed, but his tone was sulky.

"Go to your room," Daniel said.

"But I didn't get any ice cream," he began.

"Now."

Samuel ran up the stairs to his room, and they all heard him slam the door. Footsteps stomped across the ceiling, and then there was a thud as he must have thrown himself on his bed.

Maedels weren't the only ones who could be dramatic, Daniel thought. "I'm sorry," he told Ruby.

"It's allrecht. Really. That sort of thing doesn't bother me. Remember, I grew up with a Bruder."

"My best friend Hannah Rose has two Bruders. I can't imagine having more than one," Mary said with a shudder.

Ruby smiled at the horror in Mary's voice. "Ya. It can't be easy for Hannah Rose." She got up from the table. "Excuse me. I'm going to go wash my hands."

"Let me show you where the bathroom is," Mary said and jumped up from her chair.

Daniel walked over to the stove and turned on the flame under the percolator he'd filled earlier. He didn't do it to eavesdrop on the conversation Mary had with Ruby, but his Dochder's voice was clear and high with excitement and carried back to him.

"Did you mean it? That you would teach me how to bake?"

"I would love to. I'm staying with Leah for a while, you know."

Mary nodded, then frowned. "I know. Daedi says she's sick, but she's going to the doctor to get better. She's going to get better, isn't she?"

He winced at the fear he heard in Mary's voice.

"I hope so with all my heart," he heard Ruby say. "I love her, and I can see you do too. So we'll do everything we can to help her when she needs it and when she lets us. Leah is a stubborn woman who doesn't think she needs help."

Mary nodded and gave her a tentative smile. "She and Daedi were arguing once, and he told her she was stubborn. And she told him he was too." Now she giggled. "They just stood there and glared at each other."

That was enough. "Mary!" he called.

"Gotta go. There's the bathroom," she told Ruby.

Mary returned and, after she sat, began eating her ice cream. Daniel wanted to tell her that she shouldn't share a personal conversation as she had just done, but that would have to wait until after Leah and Ruby were gone.

A few minutes later, Ruby walked back into the kitchen.

"Again, I'm sorry for Samuel's behavior," Daniel told Ruby. He couldn't look at her as he remembered what his mouthy Dochder had told her.

Ruby slipped into her chair. "Please don't be concerned. No harm done. As I said, I have a Bruder. He considered it his duty to torture me."

Leah nodded. "He schur did."

"Ruby, would you like some strawberry ice cream?" Mary asked her.

"Ya, that's my favorite."

Mary nodded. "I know. Leah told me."

Daniel concentrated on eating his ice cream and realized that was why Mary had asked him to buy it. The question was why she wanted to buy Ruby's favorite and not Leah's.

He glanced up after a minute and saw Ruby looking at the ceiling. When she realized he saw her, she shrugged.

"It really was a small thing compared to what my Bruder did," she said. "I finally had enough the day I caught him putting a snake in my bed."

"A snake!" Mary dropped her spoon in her bowl, and it clattered.

Ruby nodded. "That was the last straw for me. I'd gotten tired of all his pranks and then his apologies and promises to stop.

It didn't matter that I wasn't afraid of the harmless little garter snake he'd gotten out of the Familye kitchen garden. I didn't want some dirty snake in my bed. And who knew what he'd do next? So I screamed bloody murder, and my Eldres came running and punished my Bruder."

"He was a mischievous Bu, for schur," Leah said.

"Leah had me spend the night with her a lot back then."

"I enjoyed having you," Leah said as she pushed away her empty bowl. "Well, that was a delicious meal, Mary. You did a wunderbaar job."

"You did indeed," Ruby told her. "Thank you so much for inviting me."

"You're *wilkumm*." Mary bit her lip. "When can you show me how to bake?"

"Mary."

Ruby looked at Daniel. "It's allrecht. She's eager to learn." She turned to Mary. "You could come over to Leah's after Schul and your afternoon chores."

"Well, I think after all that work, you and I should go for a walk," Leah told Mary.

"I can do the dishes," Ruby said.

"Guests don't—" Daniel began.

"Oh, nonsense," Leah interrupted him. "The two of you worked so hard. And you still have to take care of the evening chores in the barn."

Ruby rose and walked to the sink. "Might as well let her have her way," she told Daniel lightly. "You know she's going to get it."

He sighed. "Shouldn't let her get it."

But Leah and Mary were already walking out the door.

Daniel stood there, staring at Ruby's back as she turned on the faucet and squirted dish-washing liquid into the sink. He hadn't expected Leah or Ruby to do the dishes and didn't quite know what to do. Should he offer to help?

Ruby took the decision out of his hands. She turned and smiled at him. "Go handle your chores. This'll take no time."

"I'll be out in the barn," he told her and escaped.

CHAPTER SEVEN

Ruby looked out the window as she stood at the sink. She could see Daniel walking to the barn.

As if he knew she watched him, he turned and looked back, so she quickly bent her head and concentrated on the dishes. When she glanced up again, he was opening the door to the barn and going inside.

It had been a pleasant evening having supper here in his home. He and Mary had gone to a lot of trouble to do something nice for Leah, whom they clearly loved. They didn't have to invite her, but it was nice that they had done so. She used a sponge to scrub at a plate, rinsed it, then put it in the drainer.

She'd enjoyed having a meal here. It was obvious that Daniel was a loving Dat who was doing his best to raise his Kinna to be responsible and well behaved. Mary was already doing very well, cooking and being courteous and considerate. And Samuel? She smiled. Daniel shouldn't have gotten so upset at his son's antics. Ruby had been sincere in what she'd said about her Bruder's behavior when they were growing up. Oddly, she suddenly missed her Bruder. She hadn't talked to him for weeks. Maybe she'd call him later.

Ruby was halfway through the sinkful of dishes when Daniel came back. He cast her a brief glance. "I need to wash up; then I'll help dry," he said before striding toward the bathroom.

She opened her mouth to tell him he didn't need to bother, but he was already gone.

When he returned, he got a clean dish towel from a drawer and began drying the dishes and putting them into a cupboard. She felt a little uncomfortable with him standing so near. Prickles of awareness danced over her skin as she watched his strong hands wipe a dish dry. When he finished those in the drainer, he looked at her and reached for the dish she'd just rinsed. She nearly fumbled it as he took it from her.

"You must be very proud of Mary," she said, feeling awkward. "She did quite a nice job cooking and making Leah and I feel wil-kumm this evening."

"Samuel, on the other hand . . . ," he began, then trailed off.

"Don't be too hard on him," she told him, shaking her head. "He's a six-year-old Bu." She rinsed another dish, then looked at him as she handed it over. "I know it's been a while, but do you remember being six? You were years ahead of me in Schul, but I remember hearing about some of the mischief you got into."

"I don't think I was quite the mischief-maker Samuel is."

She glanced at him. "I'm schur it's not easy raising Kinna," she said quietly.

He stiffened, wary. It was what too many Maedels said before they hinted they'd like to help him with the burden. But she didn't say more and continued to do the dishes.

"Why do you keep looking out the window?" he asked when he noticed her do it for the third time.

"I hope Leah doesn't overdo things," she said after a moment. "She felt unwell after her treatment this morning. But she said she rested and felt fine and wanted to come here this evening."

"She's stubborn," he said, then remembered what he'd over-heard Mary telling her.

They glanced up in unison as they heard feet thump above. Then footsteps padded toward the staircase and down the top stairs.

"Daed? Can I come down?"

Daniel turned and looked over at Samuel, who had stopped on the stairs. "That depends. What do you want?"

"I'm hungerich."

"We just ate supper."

"I didn't get enough to eat."

"He was inviting Mr. Frog inside, remember?" she leaned over and whispered in Daniel's ear, then panicked when he turned and their faces were too close. He stared deep into her eyes, unnerving her. She drew back and cleared her throat, studiously scrubbing at a nonexistent spot on the dish.

"Careful, you'll rub off the design," he said, and she thought she heard humor in his voice.

She handed him the last dish and then put the pots in the sink. "I can make him a snack while these soak. Maybe a PB&J?"

He considered that for a long moment and then nodded. "I'll take care of the pots," he told her. "Samuel, komm and sit at the table." He gathered the ingredients for the sandwich and set them on the table, then went to the cupboard for a plate.

Samuel crept down the stairs and took a seat, looking chastened. He cast a wary glance at his Dat's back, at the sink scrubbing pots, then a hopeful one at Ruby as she began spreading peanut butter on one slice of bread, jelly on the other. She put them together, cut the sandwich into four squares, and pushed the plate toward him. Then she poured Samuel a glass of milk.

"Danki, Ruby," he said without being prompted by his Dat.

"You're wilkumm," she said as she put the jug of milk back in the refrigerator. She walked back to the sink, picked up the dish towel, and waited for Daniel to hand her a pot to dry.

Leah and Mary returned a few minutes later. Ruby thought the two exchanged a look she couldn't interpret when they saw her and Daniel together at the sink.

Ruby frowned when she saw how tired and pale Leah looked. "Leah, are you ready to go home?" She was shocked when Leah nodded.

They thanked their hosts, said their goodbyes, and then walked home. Leah stumbled on the back porch steps, and Ruby grabbed her arm to prevent her from falling.

"The walk tired me out a little more than I thought it would," Leah admitted when they went inside the house. "I let Mary set the pace, and she was still full of energy and excitement after cooking for us."

She chuckled. "Oh, if only we could tap into the energy of Kinna. Why don't you go on up and get ready for bed, and I'll bring you a cup of chamomile tea?"

"You're treating me like an old lady," Leah complained, and then she sighed. "I *am* an old lady. Ya, a cup of chamomile would be lovely. I don't think I'll have any trouble sleeping tonight, but the tea is so calming. Danki, Ruby."

Ruby made a cup of tea for both of them and carried them upstairs. Leah had changed into a nightgown and removed her Kapp. She was sitting on the side of the bed, staring at some spots on her arm, and didn't manage to pull the sleeve down before Ruby saw and frowned.

"Don't start fussing," she said briskly. "I asked the doctor about them, and he said it's a symptom some get and not to be worried."

Ruby was more concerned that Leah looked so tired. She set the tea on the bedside table and bent to kiss Leah's cheek. "Sleep well, and call me if you need me."

"I will."

She went into her room and put her tea on the bedside table, then changed into a nightgown. After she removed her Kapp, she brushed her hair out and quickly braided it.

It was nice to finally settle into bed with the tea and think about her evening.

And the undeniable attraction she had felt standing next to Daniel at the sink.

She sighed and sipped her tea and couldn't help wishing that he'd shown that he felt something. But why would he? For years, he'd only had eyes for Sadie—such a lovely Maedel, with her honey-blonde hair and big blue eyes. Even now, years after Sadie was gone, Ruby was schur Daniel only saw her as the brown-haired, brown-eyed mouse that she was.

Her gaze went to the blue dress she'd worn tonight. She'd hung it on a peg on the wall rather than putting it in her closet so that she could look at it a little while longer. Wearing it had made her feel pretty, just as the rose-colored one had done the other day when she'd worn it to accompany Leah for her oncologist appointment. Ruby had figured dressing up in it would boost her spirits. Going for such an appointment—even though it wasn't for herself—wasn't the easiest thing.

Leah had left her in the waiting room and walked back with the nurse, and her Aenti had looked so unafraid. Ruby had put on a cheerful face for her, but the moment the door closed behind them, her smile had faded, and she'd slumped in the plastic chair in the waiting room.

Now, as she lay in the narrow bed she'd slept in during sleepovers in the guest room for years, she felt like a little Kinner again, wanting the chemo to be over and for Leah to be all well and nothing bad to happen. Her eyes filled with tears, and she furiously blinked them away. It was selfish thinking about herself—and more, not believing that God knew what was best for all His Kinna.

So she blinked back the tears and prayed for Leah, and then she laid her head on her pillow and slept.

Daniel found an excuse to check in with Leah the next day, worried by what Ruby had told him about her not doing so well after her treatment.

She was walking the fields with Gideon. She reminded him of a bright-eyed little bird chattering away as they examined new growth. When she spotted him, she waved, turned to Gideon and spoke quickly with him, then walked over to talk to Daniel.

"You look well," he told her.

"I feel well."

"Ruby told me you felt rough after your treatment yesterday."

Leah waved her hand. "Ruby worries too much. I rested, and you saw that I was fine last night."

"You were very tired after your walk with Mary," he reminded her. "And Ruby doesn't worry too much. She just wants you to get well. She loves you. We all do."

"And I love all of you." She raised her face to the sun, closed her eyes for a moment, and basked in the warmth. Then she opened them and looked at him. "It's a glorious day God gave us today."

"You say that every day."

"It's true every day. Especially these days."

Daniel stood there and stared at her as her words sank in. Although the day was warm for spring, he felt a chill. "Leah, you're going to be allrecht."

"Of course I am," she said confidently. "Let's go inside. I want to get something to drink."

They walked into her house, and she put the kettle on to boil. While they waited, she took cookies from the jar and set a plate of them before him as he sat at the table. When he didn't immediately reach for one, her eyebrows went up.

"What? No cookies? Are you getting too many from the Maedels?" she teased.

He felt himself redden. It was a common practice for young unmarried women to take baked goods to the single men they were interested in—especially before marriage season. He supposed they truly felt the way to a man's heart was through his stomach. . . . Well, he hoped he wasn't so shallow that he would marry someone because he liked her cooking.

Had Mary told Leah that several Maedels had brought him cookies this week?

He didn't feel much like eating after what they'd just discussed in the fields, but he chose one and bit in.

Leah took the kettle from the stove when it whistled, poured two mugs of hot water, and carried them to the table. He chose a tea bag from the little box of them on the table and dipped it in the water over and over again.

"You make your tea as black as coffee," she said after she dipped her tea bag just twice. "Are you schur you don't want me to make you some coffee?"

He shook his head. "Had two cups already this morning." He glanced around. "Where's Ruby?"

"She's visiting her Mudder. She'll be back before your Kinna come home from Schul, so don't forget to send them over after chores."

"As if Mary would let me forget."

"I think Samuel wants to come too. He was mischievous last night to get attention, but I don't think he dislikes Ruby."

He stirred two teaspoons of sugar into his tea. "I hope not because I won't have him behaving that way to anyone."

"Kinna do sometimes have a strong reaction to a new person in their Eldre's life when they start dating," she said thoughtfully, then sipped her tea.

"I'm not ready to date."

"So you've said. Sometimes the right person comes along when we think we're not ready. And don't go rolling your eyes at me. That happened with Eli and me. I had been so busy helping my Mudder take care of Kinna—she had ten, as you know—that I wanted some time before I'd marry and start a Familye of my own. But we don't control these things."

She gazed out the window, but it seemed to him that she was looking inward rather than at something outside.

"Leah?"

"Hmm?" She dragged her attention back to him.

"You seem distracted. Would you like me to go?"

She shook her head. "Nee. Sorry. I just was remembering how Eli made me change my mind about the direction of my life." She sighed. "Oh, I miss him so."

"Me too. He taught me so much about farming. But more important, he was a Dat to me after mine died."

She clasped his hand. "He loved you like a Sohn."

Daniel wondered if either of them had ever regretted that they hadn't had Kinna of their own. But it wasn't a question one asked.

"Listen, I promised Eli I would help you in any way I could. We haven't gone over this month's bills yet. Do you feel like doing that now?"

She chuckled. "I don't feel like doing it at any time, but I will. It's a lot more pleasant a task when we do it together."

So they worked on the farm books, and she wrote out checks. First and most important was one for Gideon. She placed that one on the table, then wrote the rest, slipped them into envelopes, and put stamps on them.

Daniel stacked them up and took a deposit slip from her to take to the bank.

"Thanks for the help," she said, leaning back in her chair and looking tired. "*All* of the help. I don't know what I'd have done without you these past years."

He closed the farm book and looked at her. "It's been my pleasure. Listen, Leah, are you schur you want to stick with our arrangement?"

"Why wouldn't I?"

"Well, Ruby has been doing so much for you, I figured maybe you'd want to consider changing things. I'd understand."

"There's no—" She broke off at a tap on the door, and then Gideon walked inside.

"Leah, Daniel, got a minute? I'd like one of you to take a look at Ned's leg. He was limping when I led him out to pasture so that I could clean his stall."

"You go, if you don't mind," Leah told Daniel. "You have a better sense of what's wrong with horses than I do."

"Not true," he said. "But I'm happy to take a look and then report back to you." He rose, picked up the check, and handed it to Gideon. "I'll see you later, Leah. Get some rest."

He walked out to the pasture to check on Ned and saw that Gideon had been right to be concerned. They bandaged the horse's leg, and then Daniel headed to his house. He had a lot to do and wanted to make schur he was done before the Kinna came home. He'd probably only have a few minutes to spend with them before they'd go rushing off to bake with Ruby.

At least this time, any baked treats would be brought over by his Dochder and Sohn—not some Maedel hoping to interest him in asking her out.

CHAPTER EIGHT

Ruby grinned when she heard the ruckus at the back door.

There was a volley of knocks before the door opened and Mary and Samuel stuck their faces in.

"Hi, Ruby!" they chorused.

She laughed. "Komm, I've been waiting for you." She watched as Samuel started to shove his way ahead of Mary and then appeared to think better of it and stood back to let her walk in first.

Mary carried a small wooden box in her hands as if it was a precious possession. She set it down on the kitchen table. "I brought Mamm's recipe box so that we could make her biscuits."

"That's *gut.* I remember how much your Dat liked them."

She lifted the lid, drew out the recipe card, and handed it to Ruby. "Should I get the flour and the other ingredients from our house?"

Ruby shook her head. "I have plenty." She waved her hand at the canister of flour she'd set out with a big ceramic bowl on the counter. "Let's wash our hands and get started."

They did as she asked while Ruby studied the recipe card. The recipe looked very similar to the one she made, but Mary wanted to make the biscuits the way her Mudder had, so that's what they would do.

"Samuel, after Mary and I make the biscuits, we can make some snickerdoodles. In the meantime, you know where Leah keeps art materials for you, so you can get those out of the drawer if you want."

"Danki," he said politely, then went to the drawer and pulled out paper and crayons.

"Where's Leah?"

"She's resting, but she'll be down soon," Ruby said after a glance at the clock. She set the oven to the proper temperature and then joined Mary at the counter. "The most important thing to remember about baking is that you have to be much more careful about sticking to the recipe. You can't just eyeball things."

"Eyeball? You're putting eyeballs in something?" Samuel asked, standing up in his chair to see better.

"It's an expression," Ruby said quickly. "It means you don't measure exactly; you look at it with your eyes and decide how much of some ingredient to use."

"Sit down, Samuel," Mary said with her most authoritative, big-Schweschder voice. "You know Daed says not to stand on a chair."

He stuck his tongue out at her, but he sat and went back to coloring.

"You see, if you decided just to judge how much salt to use instead of measuring it, you might end up with salty biscuits," Ruby went on. "So just be sure you measure carefully when you bake."

She showed Mary how to scoop a cup of flour from the canister and then use a plastic knife to level off the excess. Mary dumped the flour into the bowl, then measured and added the other dry ingredients the same way. Then Ruby showed Mary how to cut in the cold butter until it was the size of tiny peas. Buttermilk came next, and Mary had to work hard to combine everything until it was a sticky dough.

The next step involved turning it out on a floured countertop and kneading it gently. Ruby explained how folding the dough over and over onto itself helped make layers that would be flaky after baking. Mary cut out the biscuits and placed them in a baking pan, and Ruby put the pan in the oven.

"I always set the timer for a couple of minutes less than the recipe says and give them a quick check," she told Mary. "Ovens can be different, too, so it may take a little more time—or a little less—using the one at your house."

They cleaned up the bowl, utensils, and counter surface while the biscuits baked. Then Ruby had Samuel get the recipe card for snickerdoodles and assembled everything they'd need to make them.

He stood on a stool to better reach the counter and carefully measured the ingredients she handed him. Ruby hadn't thought he'd been watching his Schweschder while she worked, but apparently, he had. He knew how to use the plastic knife to scrape off excess flour from the measuring cup before he dumped it into the bowl.

"So you like snickerdoodles better than other cookies?"

He nodded and frowned, concentrating on mixing the dough with a big wooden spoon. When it came time to roll little balls of dough in cinnamon sugar, she wondered if that was why he liked these cookies best. He carefully placed each ball on a baking sheet and then, at her direction, pushed his thumb in the center so that they wouldn't puff too much while baking. They were ready to slide into the oven when the timer went off and Ruby pulled the biscuits out.

She'd no sooner placed the biscuits on top of the stove when she heard sniffling. Turning, she saw tears running down Mary's cheeks.

"Oh, Lieb, what's wrong?" she asked gently as she reached for a paper napkin from the basket on the table and wiped away Mary's tears.

"They look just like Mamm's," Mary told her as she gazed at the golden-brown biscuits.

"That's *gut*, right?"

"I guess." She took a shaky breath.

"Let's sit down and try one and see how they taste," Ruby suggested.

They split the biscuits and spread them with butter before sampling them.

"It tastes just like Mamm's," Mary said, and her eyes filled with tears again.

"I think she'd be very happy you did such a *gut* job. And that you remembered her for the times she made something you enjoyed."

The timer went off again, and Ruby took the baking sheet from the oven. She transferred the cookies to a cooling rack and then placed a couple on a plate and set them on the table.

"Smells just like Mamm did when she baked," Samuel said as he picked up a cookie and inhaled the scent of cinnamon and sugar. His mouth trembled. "Like cinnamum."

Ruby's heart ached for the Kinna. Who knew the baking lesson would be so bittersweet for them?

She was relieved when Leah descended the stairs and walked into the kitchen. "Something smells so delicious!" she cried. "Do I get to be a taste tester?"

When the Maedel appeared at his doorstep bearing a plate of warm, fragrant baked goods, Daniel couldn't resist inviting her in.

"Please, komm in," he said, and she walked in, beaming.

"I wanted you to have some right away," Mary told him as she held out the plate. "While they're hot."

Daniel had checked the menu posted on the refrigerator and had been thinking about starting supper, but he closed the door and immediately sat down at the kitchen table.

"I can't wait." He smiled as she put the plate in front of him and broke open a biscuit. Fragrant steam poured out. It brought back the memory of Sadie's biscuits. He buttered one half, bit in, and chewed. Tasted exactly like hers too. "So *gut*. You know what this means, don't you?"

She shook her head.

"You're going to have to make them a lot now." He finished the first half and buttered the other before popping it into his mouth. "Just so delicious," he told her.

"Daedi, you're not supposed to talk with your mouth full!" she told him and laughed.

"Come here," he said, holding out his arms. When she went into them, he hugged her tight. "I'm proud of you. You did such a *gut* job the very first time."

"Danki. I liked baking with Ruby. She makes it fun." She pulled away. "I gotta go back and have some of Samuel's snickerdoodles."

"I hope I get to taste test those too."

There was a thump at the door. Mary hurried over to open it and found Samuel standing there with a plate of cookies in his hands.

"I didn't want to drop any," he said as he walked in. "I brought you some, Daedi. They're just like Mamm's."

Daniel accepted the cookie Samuel handed him and took a bite. "Wow. Delicious, Samuel." He chewed, then swallowed. "Well, I'd say that was a great baking lesson. Can't wait for the two of you to make more here in our kitchen."

He started to take a bite of a second cookie, and then he realized that although Mary was smiling, there were signs of tears on her cheeks. "Mary, what's wrong?"

She stared at the floor and shook her head. And didn't answer him for a long moment. "I got sad when Ruby got the biscuits out of the oven and they looked just like Mamm's," she admitted, and she lifted her eyes to him. "It made me miss her."

Daniel felt a stab of pain in his heart. He held out his arms. She rushed into them, and he hugged her.

"My cookies smell like Mamm," Samuel spoke up.

Then he was nudging at Daniel's arm, and Daniel embraced him as well. "I miss her too. But in a way, it's *gut* when we miss someone after they're gone. It means we loved them."

They stayed like that—a unit—until finally, Mary drew back. "We need to go back and help Ruby clean up."

He nodded. "Remember to thank her."

They left, and he sat there for a moment and felt a little tug of guilt. It was another reminder of how they missed their Mudder. Oh, he knew it wasn't his fault. The driver of the automobile had been responsible—not him. But he still felt vaguely guilty that they had enjoyed being with Ruby and shared not only a baking lesson but some of the emotions they were feeling about their Mudder.

He missed the companionship of having a Fraa, of knowing that there was someone who loved him and supported what he did and made a Familye with him. Who wanted to look toward the future with him.

Well, sitting there thinking about what he didn't have in his life wasn't helping anything, he knew. The Kinna would be home soon and wanting their supper. And there were chores. There were always chores.

With a sigh, he got up and went back to the refrigerator. Tonight's menu was supposed to be meatloaf. He got out the hamburger and the other ingredients he needed and had it in the oven with some potatoes and carrots when Mary and Samuel returned.

"We made enough biscuits for supper for everyone," Mary told him as she handed him the basket.

Daniel peeled back the checked cloth that covered golden-brown biscuits, still warm from the oven. He quickly covered it again and set it at the back of the stove.

The cookies Samuel carried went into the ceramic pig cookie jar, over the protests his Sohn made that he wanted "just one more."

"No spoiling your supper."

"That's what Ruby said," Samuel complained.

"When he wanted a fourth cookie," Mary told him.

"How many biscuits did you eat?" Samuel demanded, and they were off on a spirited debate.

"Enough," Daniel spoke over the din. "Chores."

They quieted and followed him out to the barn. Sometimes Daniel felt that teaching the Kinna how to do things took more patience than he had—and twice the time it took if he did them himself. But they needed to learn what to do, and on a farm, everyone had to pull their weight.

Feeding and watering the horses were their favorite chores. It had been the same with him. They measured out the grain—at first, Samuel had wanted to give them more than they should have. He'd had to explain that just as Samuel had gotten sick with a stomachache when he insisted on eating too many hot dogs, even animals as big as horses would get sick with a stomachache—or worse, diarrhea—if they were fed too much.

Mary stroked the nose of Star, her favorite, and talked quietly to her. Daniel had the suspicion that Mary was the horse's favorite of the two because she was gentler. And she always remembered to bring apples as a treat.

Daniel cut the apples and gave pieces to Mary and Samuel to feed to the horses. Then they walked back to the house. The oven timer was going off just as they stepped into the kitchen.

They washed up, and he pulled the pan out and placed it on the back of the stove while Mary set the table and Samuel filled glasses with water.

Both Kinna chattered nonstop about their baking lesson during supper. Daniel realized that learning to bake had taught them a little about following directions, arithmetic, and cooperation.

Mary beamed as Daniel ate two biscuits and praised them again. They had Samuel's cookies for dessert. Daniel ate several with a cup of coffee and thought again that his Kinna were growing up too fast.

"Oh no!" Mary cried suddenly. "I forgot the recipe box! I have to go get it!"

"I'm schur it'll be fine at Leah's until tomorrow."

"Please, I hafta go get it," Mary implored. "It's still early. Leah won't be in bed."

Daniel sighed, then nodded. "Komm right back. We have dishes to wash and baths to take."

He and Samuel cleared the table, and then he sent his Sohn to take his bath. Samuel was still a little too careless with things that were breakable to trust him with washing them. Then Daniel thought about it and went upstairs to make schur that Samuel wasn't overfilling the tub. He hadn't forgotten the time he'd trusted Samuel and then, when he checked on him, found the tub overflowing. He'd had to wade through a foot of water to turn off the faucet and then mop the floor. Fortunately, the incident hadn't caused damage to the wooden planks.

This time, Samuel glanced up at him with a look of innocence as he sat in the tub. But there were a lot of bubbles surrounding him.

Daniel frowned. "Mary's not going to be happy you used her bubble bath."

"Just a little."

"Use some soap," Daniel told him as he handed him a washcloth. "And don't poke around if you want to read a story before bed."

Mary had returned when Daniel went downstairs. She stood at the sink, washing the dishes.

He picked up a dish towel, took the dish she rinsed, and began drying it. "Your Bruder's in the tub."

She wrinkled her nose. "That means I have to scrub it before I take my bath. You remember the time we found the frog in there with him."

"He didn't this time," Daniel told her. But now that he thought about it, he hadn't looked really hard. There had been a lot of bubbles. Surely he hadn't put a frog in with him. . . .

"Tell you what, I'll go up and scrub the tub as soon as I dry the dishes." As he went to put a plate in the cupboard, he saw that the recipe box was back in its usual place near the stove.

"Ruby said we could come over again one afternoon for another baking lesson if we want," Mary told him as she handed him a plate. "Can we, Daedi? I had fun, and Samuel did too."

When he hesitated, she turned to look at him. "Leah said she enjoyed what we made and hoped we'd come again."

Mary had her Mudder's eyes and the same way of looking at him when she wanted something. He'd never been able to resist Sadie, either.

"I guess, as long as you don't make a pest of yourself."

"*I'm* not the pest," she said loftily. She cast her gaze toward the ceiling.

"I think it's time to get Samuel out of the tub." He set the dish towel down and started for the stairs. It was entirely too quiet. And when it was quiet and Samuel wasn't in direct eyesight, well, it wasn't a *gut* thing. He took the steps two at a time.

CHAPTER NINE

Ruby heard a knock at the kitchen door, and then it opened.

"*Guder Mariye*," Daniel said and stepped inside. He held out two plates.

She took them and set them on the counter. "Danki." She wondered why he hadn't just sent them with the Kinna yesterday when they'd come for another baking lesson. "Would you like some coffee? I just made a pot."

"Nee, Danki. Mary's been coming over here a lot. I don't want her to make a pest of herself."

Ruby frowned. "Mary could never be a pest. Neither could Samuel."

"Samuel's been over here too?"

"Just twice. For a few minutes. He wasn't as interested in baking after the snickerdoodles."

The oven timer went off. She grabbed potholders and pulled a pan of cinnamon rolls out of the oven, then set them on a rack to cool. When she saw his glance slide toward the rolls, she smiled inwardly. He'd turned down coffee, but could he turn down fresh-baked cinnamon rolls?

But he determinedly looked away from them and met her gaze. "I'm just concerned she could get . . . attached."

"Attached?"

Looking mildly frustrated, he took off his straw hat and ran a hand through his hair. "I know Mary misses her Mudder. I wouldn't want her to form an attachment to you and be hurt."

"How would I hurt her?"

"I'm not looking for a Fraa—"

"Well, you don't need to worry because I'm not looking for a Mann!"

Highly offended, she turned back to the bowl of confectioner's sugar she'd set on the counter. Ignoring him, she added a little hot water from the tea kettle to the bowl and began beating the icing with a wooden spoon. Hard.

"I don't mean to offend—"

"Well, for not meaning to, you do a *gut* job! Excuse me. I have work to do." She kept her back to him and drizzled the icing over the warm rolls. She blinked hard at tears, angry and a little surprised at how she'd spoken to him. It took a lot to rile her, but he'd managed it nicely.

When she heard the door shut, she turned to make schur he was gone.

"Did I hear Daniel?" Leah asked as she descended the stairs and walked into the kitchen.

"Ya."

"What's wrong?"

"Daniel seemed to think he needed to warn me he's not interested in finding a Fraa."

"Oh?" Leah's mouth quirked into a grin as she poured herself a cup of coffee. "Wonder what brought that on?"

Ruby finished the icing and carried the pan over to the kitchen table. "He said he was concerned about Mary coming over so often."

She fetched two plates and served them each a roll, adding scrambled eggs she'd kept warm until Leah got up. For once, her Aenti had slept in a little. Ruby thought she still looked a little wan. "I hope we didn't wake you."

"Nee, but I'd like to have been there for your reaction. You still have smoke coming out of your ears."

A laugh escaped her. "I think he knows I'm not interested."

Leah sipped her coffee and studied her. "I won't make excuses for Daniel—"

"*Gut!*"

"But I think he's just being overprotective."

Ruby stared down at her plate, then up at Leah. "The last thing I'd do is hurt his Kinna."

Leah reached over and squeezed her hand. "I know that. Sometimes men just don't know how to say things. He's told me he knows his Kinna miss having a Mudder, but he's not ready to remarry. I think he feels a little guilty about it."

She paused as she picked up her roll and bit into it. "Tell me, did he actually leave here without having a roll?"

Laughing, Ruby nodded. "You can see there are only two rolls missing from the pan."

"I don't see how he managed it," Leah said. "Cinnamon rolls are a favorite of his. It must have been hard for him."

Ruby bit back a smile. "If he lets Mary come over to bake some, I may persuade her to bake something else." She set down her fork. "Nee, I'm not that petty."

"Of course you're not." Leah's eyes twinkled. "But you should put the leftovers from this pan in the breadbox. Daniel has a habit of stopping over for coffee with me most mornings." She pushed aside her plate.

Ruby stood and took their plates to the sink and was happy to see that Leah had eaten most of what she'd served her.

"I heard there's a singing after church tomorrow. You haven't been out of the house much since you moved in."

"I don't know."

"You're young. You need to have some fun."

Ruby remembered the last singing. She hadn't had much fun attending it.

"Eli and I went to many a singing when we were courting," Leah said, reminiscing. "The best part was taking the long way home afterward."

Stories like that warmed Ruby's heart. She wanted a relationship like the one she'd seen Leah and Eli have. Her Eldres too. Whenever she saw Daniel and Sadie at church and other events, she'd noticed that they had seemed very happy, so it was no surprise to her that he hadn't rushed to remarry.

"Well." Leah shook her head as if to dispel memories, then looked at Ruby. "So are you going to go?"

"Go?"

"To the singing."

"I don't know. I'll think about it tomorrow." She walked to the sink to wash the dishes and debated what to make for a dessert for the afternoon's sewing circle. After she had an apple streusel coffee cake in the oven, she went into the living room to make sure it was tidy.

Time passed quickly. Soon the sewing-circle members were arriving, and the house filled with bright, happy chatter. Her Mudder and Schweschder, Emma, came, and she was so happy to see them. She'd only had time for quick visits home and a conversation after church since she'd moved in with Leah.

Several of the women complimented Ruby on the wedding ring quilt. She was nearly finished with it and hoped to take it to the quilt shop in town to let Lillian offer it for sale. Then she and Lillian would talk about what pattern the next quilt should be.

Sarah came a little while later, and she and Ruby sat next to each other and caught up on things.

"The doctor told Daed he's in remission from his cancer," she told Ruby. "Is Leah doing as well as she seems to be?"

"I think so." She wished she could say Leah was in remission. "I'm sorry we haven't seen each other much. I don't like to leave Leah by herself."

Sarah nodded. "I stay with Daed when Mamm needs to leave the house." She leaned closer. "So maybe you'll get to know Daniel better now that you're living next to him," Sarah whispered. "He's so handsome."

Ruby didn't want to discuss Daniel. She glanced around and then set her sewing aside. "I'll be right back. I need to see to the refreshments."

"I can help."

"Nee, I've got it under control," she said quickly. She left the group sewing in the living room and slipped into the kitchen to make more coffee and tea.

"Thought I'd see if you needed some help," Emma said as she walked into the room.

She went straight for the desserts on the table and chose a brownie. "Mmm, I can tell these are yours," she said, her mouth full. "You make the best brownies." She wandered over to the counter and picked up a mug.

"Want some coffee with that?"

Emma shook her head. "Can't have more than one cup of coffee a day now," Emma said, then grinned. "I'm pregnant."

Thrilled, Ruby hugged her. "I thought you were glowing lately."

"I feel *gut*. No morning sickness." She finished the brownie and glanced at the table. "I have to have another. After all, I'm eating for two."

Ruby didn't think that meant she should have two brownies. But she stayed silent as she fixed her Schweschder a cup of tea and hugged her again. "Go on and sit down with the others. I can handle things here."

She served coffee and tea and took empty cups and dessert plates back to set in the sink just as Daniel came in the back door with his Dochder.

"Mary saw all the buggies and was wondering if she could attend the sewing circle," Daniel said.

"Of course," Ruby responded with a smile for the Kinner. "Are you wanting to learn to sew?"

Mary nodded shyly.

"Maybe you'd like to make a crib quilt for your dolls. That was my first sewing project."

"Ya!"

"Help yourself to a dessert and go on into the living room. I'll be right there."

"I know Leah's busy with the women sewing," Daniel told Ruby as Mary chose a cookie and left the room. "Can you make schur she gets this?" He handed her an envelope with a bank logo on it.

Ruby accepted it and tucked it into the pocket of her apron. And didn't miss his glance at the array of sweet treats on the table.

"Help yourself to something," she said. "There are cinnamon rolls in the breadbox." She couldn't resist since Leah had told her they were a favorite of Daniel's, and Mary had mentioned wanting to learn to make them for her dad as well.

She saw him glance in its direction as she turned the flame up under the percolator. *Let's see if he can resist my cinnamon rolls,* she thought with an inward smile.

He took two on his way out.

When she returned to the living room, she found Mary sitting next to her Mudder. Miriam was helping her to choose some scraps of fabric, just as she and Leah had done when she was a Kinner. So Ruby settled into a chair with her own quilt and watched the next generation learn the old craft of making something beautiful and useful for the home.

It felt so nice to have the time to enjoy being part of the sewing circle when she hadn't been able to because of her job for so long.

Daniel sat on his porch after Sunday-evening supper and took a little time to himself before he had to get the Kinna ready for bed.

He caught a movement out of the corner of his eye and watched Ruby leave Leah's house and begin walking down the road, carrying a basket topped with a cloth. From the direction she was headed and the fact that she was wearing one of the new dresses she'd made, he figured she was going to the singing.

Leah had urged him to attend when he talked to her the day before, but he wanted nothing to do with it. Singings were part of his past—something he had done when he was courting Sadie. He was twenty-eight now, and as someone who'd been married and widowed, he felt too old for such a thing. He'd told Leah it was for singles, and she'd relented. Now he wondered if Leah had hoped he and Ruby would attend together.

Well, he'd made it clear to Ruby that he wasn't interested in getting remarried. He winced as he remembered how quickly and firmly she'd let him know she wasn't interested in finding a Mann.

Her reaction had surprised him. Her eyes had flashed, and color had rushed into her cheeks, giving them a lovely rose color. She wasn't the quiet little mouse he'd thought she was. Remembering, he stared after her thoughtfully.

He found himself wondering what sweet treat she carried in that basket. He'd taken her offer of cinnamon rolls yesterday and thought they were the best he'd ever tasted. Then he felt a little guilty. Sadie had been a wunderbaar baker.

Well, maybe Mary would learn to make them next, and he wouldn't have to be without his favorite baked treat.

But you said you didn't want her to be a pest, his conscience reminded him.

Ouch.

He was glad Ruby had quickly told him she wasn't. But he wasn't wrong to be concerned that Mary was getting attached to her. He knew Mary and Samuel missed their Mudder. And it wasn't unknown for Maedels to try to pay attention to a man's Kinna to show him their maternal side.

With a sigh, he got up. He was getting entirely too jaded.

Hours later, he walked back into the house after doing his final check of the horses in the barn. As he went through the house to close the downstairs windows and lock the front door, he happened to glance through the window next to the door and saw a buggy pull up in front of Leah's house. He frowned, wondering who was visiting so late. That wasn't one of Ruby's Eldres. That was Isaiah Miller's buggy. He recognized it because Isaiah had rigged up a *verboten* stereo system back during his *Rumschpringa* days and shown it off to Daniel and some other males. Isaiah was closer to Ruby's age than his, but judging from the sound coming from it, he hadn't disconnected the sound system.

Ruby stepped out of the buggy, and the bright full moon overhead illuminated her face. It seemed to cast an ethereal glow over her features, and then a cloud moved past, throwing shadows across her face and making her look mysterious. A slight breeze molded her dress around her slim figure as she turned and began walking up the porch steps and went into the house.

The buggy rolled on down the road, the noise faded, and the night was silent again.

Daniel shut the window and locked it and the front door. As he walked back through the house and then climbed the stairs, he wondered if Isaiah and Ruby were seeing each other. He wondered what outgoing, charming Isaiah saw in the quiet, self-effacing Ruby. Then he remembered how, shortly after he'd begun dating Sadie, other young men in the church had been interested in her.

He wondered if he was giving Ruby a second glance because another man was interested in her. Did men desire a woman more when other men pursued her? And did the reverse happen? Did young women look at a man harder if one of them was seeing someone?

He pondered that as he looked in on the Kinna and then got ready for bed.

After what felt like just minutes, he was woken up by Samuel pulling on his arm and crying.

"Daedi, Daedi, there's a monster in my room! You gotta get him!" Samuel told him tearfully.

Groaning, Daniel sat up and hugged his Sohn just as thunder rumbled and lightning flashed, illuminating the room. "It's allrecht. The storm woke you. There are no monsters in your room. C'mon, I'll show you."

Samuel clutched his hand as they walked down the hall to his room. Daniel turned on the little battery-operated lamp on the bedside table, then got down on his hands and knees and looked under the bed.

"No monsters under the bed," he announced.

"The closet." Samuel gave it a fearful look. "Look in the closet. I woke up, and there were these big spooky eyes looking out at me!" He held on to Daniel's legs as he walked over to it so that it was a halting, stilted journey that reminded Daniel of an old Frankenstein movie he'd seen on his Rumschpringa.

Daniel opened the closet door—it hadn't even been open as Samuel had claimed—and held it wide. He moved things around in it to show Samuel there were no monsters with big spooky eyes inside. Then he closed the door firmly.

"Come on, Sohn," he said. "Let's get you back in bed."

Samuel climbed in and let his Dat pull the quilt up around his shoulders. "You can keep the light on if you want, allrecht?"

"Will you stay until I go to sleep?"

He bent down to kiss Samuel's forehead. "I will. Now go to sleep. You have Schul tomorrow."

It didn't take long for Samuel to drift off to sleep. Then Daniel got up and left the room to check on Mary. He needn't have worried. Mary had never had a problem with storms or nightmares.

As he walked back to his room, he could see a light on in one of the upstairs bedrooms in Leah's house. From what he knew of the house, it wasn't Leah's bedroom, so it must be that Ruby was up. He wondered if the storm had woken her or if she was simply staying up late. While she was staying with Leah, she didn't need to get up early to go to her job.

He climbed back into bed and thought about seeing her coming home from the singing in Isaiah's buggy. She had surprised him with her passionate outburst, telling him that he didn't have to worry about her wanting to marry him. He couldn't remember a time he'd put his foot in his mouth as perfectly as that.

But now, as he remembered their encounter in Leah's kitchen, he wasn't sorry he had a chance to see the passionate woman that she could be when standing up for herself—not the somewhat shy, humble Maedel who served others like a biblical Martha whom he had known all his life.

He wondered if Isaiah had seen that woman as well.

CHAPTER TEN

"So did you have fun at the singing?" Leah asked Ruby as she cooked breakfast the next morning.

Leah had been in bed when she came home, so they hadn't talked the night before.

Ruby shrugged. "It was allrecht."

"You got a ride home with one of your friends like I told you to, didn't you?"

"Ya."

"I thought I heard music. Must have been dreaming."

She bit her lip as she flipped the last pancake onto a plate and turned the flame off under the skillet. "Isaiah gave me a ride home. He has a sound system in his buggy."

"Isaiah?" Leah ignored her pancakes and grasped Ruby's hand. "Isaiah Miller?"

"Ya." She topped her pancakes with a pat of butter, then poured on syrup.

"Ruby?"

"Hmm?" She took a bite and looked up.

"I don't want to be nosey—"

She made the mistake of chuckling, and the bite of pancake got caught going down. Leah reached over and pounded on her back. Ruby recovered and sipped from her glass of orange juice.

"Very funny," Leah said dryly. "See what you did to yourself being a smart aleck?"

"Ya, I thought it was funny." She looked at her Aenti. "I think Isaiah was just being kind, giving me a ride."

But he had looked at her differently last night and made a point of coming over to talk to her when everyone stopped for a snack midway through the singing. She felt flattered he'd paid attention to her. He was tall, blond, and blue-eyed . . . and very charming. . . .

"It's wise to take things slowly," Leah told her, and it seemed to Ruby that she chose her words carefully. "He's a nice young man."

"But?"

"No *but.*" Leah was silent for several minutes as she ate her pancakes.

"I know you like Daniel. A lot. But he's not interested in me."

"And Isaiah is?"

"I didn't say that." But after he'd dropped her off last night, she'd wondered. Ya, she'd wondered.

Leah rose and topped off their coffee. "Well, I think you're a lovely young woman, and you have many wunderbaar qualities. There will be a man who appreciates them one day. But you have to believe you are worthy before he does. You need to have more self-confidence."

Easier said than done, Ruby wanted to say.

They finished breakfast and cleaned up the kitchen and then settled down to sew—Ruby on the wedding ring quilt and Leah on a lap quilt. Ruby fretted that Leah was working on something smaller, but the size was probably better for her Aenti these days because she tired easily. Schur enough, after an hour or so, Leah decided to go read in the recliner in the living room. Ruby knew she'd find her napping before long.

Ruby told herself rest was *gut*. Rest was necessary for healing. And when she caught herself worrying, she made herself say a prayer instead. God knew what He was doing.

Daniel stopped by for his daily visit not long after Leah went into the other room.

She saw him cast a considering glance at her sewing and lift one eyebrow, and she stiffened. "I'm sewing it for sale at Lillian's quilt shop, not for when I trap a man into marriage."

"I didn't say a word," he told her, holding up his hands.

"You didn't have to." She forced her attention back to the quilt and told herself that she shouldn't have let him rile her. "Leah's in the living room. Said she wanted to read for a while, but she's probably fallen asleep by now." She sighed. "She tends to do that after a few minutes these days."

"That worries you."

"Of course it does."

He took his hat off, ran his hand through his hair, and sighed. "I worry about her too. It's times like this that can be hard to trust, to have faith."

"True."

She felt herself relenting. He was obviously not just a good neighbor but a good friend to Leah. "I can peek in the other room if you want."

"Up to you. I can come back."

Ruby rose and walked into the other room. Schur enough, Leah was sleeping peacefully. She lifted the knitted throw from the back of the sofa and tucked it around her.

When she turned to start for the kitchen, she saw Daniel standing there in the doorway with an expression on his face she couldn't read. He held a finger to his lips, nodded, then walked back into the kitchen.

"I'll stop by later," he told her when they were in the kitchen. He walked to the door and then, just as he was about to go out, turned to look at her. "Remember what Leah always says."

"Worry's arrogant," she said softly. "God knows what He's doing."

He nodded, and then he was gone.

When there was a knock on the door just minutes later, she thought he'd come back. But when he didn't enter right afterward like he always did, she got up to answer it.

"Isaiah! I wasn't expecting you."

He took off his hat as he stepped inside. "Nice quilt you're making there," he said.

"Danki. Would you like something to drink?"

"Nee, Danki. Daed sent me into town for some supplies for the job we're doing, and you were on the way. Thought I'd see if you wanted to go for a drive. Later, after supper. Maybe get some ice cream."

"I'd like that."

"Fine. Around six?"

She nodded.

"Well, see you then." He clamped his hat on his head and was gone.

Ruby took her seat and just sat there, staring at the door. A drive after supper wouldn't be as nice as the one they'd taken by moonlight last night. But he'd asked her out. It wasn't just a ride home because he thought she needed it, like she'd figured last night was.

Nee. He'd asked her out. She couldn't stop herself from smiling as she went back to sewing the quilt.

Daniel went over to Leah's after supper. The Kinna were spending the night at their *Grossmudder*'s house, so he had a little time on his hands.

He found Leah sipping a cup of tea in her kitchen. She looked up and smiled when he walked into the room. "Ruby told me you stopped by earlier."

"We didn't want to wake you."

"I was just resting my eyes."

"I heard snoring."

"You did not!"

He chuckled. "Nee. It's just fun to tease you." Then he sobered. "How are you feeling, Leah?"

"I'm fine. You don't usually come over this time of day."

"The Kinna are having a sleepover at my Mudder's house."

"Then sit. Do you want some tea? The water's probably still hot."

He shook his head. "Nee. Danki."

When he heard footsteps descending the stairs, he glanced over and saw Ruby. She looked surprised to see him but said nothing as she walked to Leah and bent to kiss her cheek. Daniel found himself studying the way her eyes sparkled and her cheeks seemed a little flushed. She was wearing the new dress he knew she'd sewn, and there was an air of suppressed excitement about her he found intriguing.

"Need anything before I go?" she asked Leah as she picked up her purse from the bench by the back door.

"Not a thing. Have a *gut* time."

"Danki. I'm going to go wait on the front porch." She gave Daniel a brief nod, then left the room.

Leah was smiling when Daniel turned his attention to her. "What?"

"She looks lovely in blue, doesn't she?"

He shifted in his chair, uncomfortable with the way she'd observed him staring at Ruby. "Stop trying to play matchmaker."

"I wasn't. Too late for that now. She's seeing Isaiah tonight. I'm afraid you lost your chance."

"Leah."

She sighed. "You can't blame me. I guess I just hoped that the two of you might get together. God never gifted Eli and me with Kinna, so Ruby sort of became the Dochder we never had. Same thing with you. We always thought of you as the Sohn we didn't have."

"Danki. You know I love you too. But Ruby and I kind of got off on the wrong foot."

"Seems to me it's easy to change that."

He shook his head. "I guess it would be if I hadn't put it in my mouth." He didn't know if the two women had talked about it, but Leah hadn't changed the way she behaved toward him.

"She's different since she's been living here," he blurted out.

Leah nodded slowly. "You noticed. Some Maedels rate a second look." She patted his hand. "Like I said, seems to me it's easy to change that. Think about it. Now, was there anything special you wanted to talk about when you came by earlier?"

"Just some farm business. Progress report I discussed with Gideon. If you're not too tired."

"Not tired at all."

"Guess that comes from resting your eyes earlier, eh?" he teased, glad that she'd changed the subject.

He went over a couple of concerns he'd discussed with Gideon. He took his promise to Eli to look after Leah seriously, and he and Gideon worked closely together to make schur the farm ran well.

"So, what will you do with yourself without the Kinna this evening?" Leah asked him when they finished.

"Maybe just enjoy the quiet. Read." He thought about it for a minute. He didn't have anything new to read. "Would you mind if I borrowed a book?"

"Help yourself. You know where they are."

"Danki. Have a *gut* evening, and give me a shout if you need anything."

He went into the living room and looked through the bookshelves there. Both Leah and Eli loved books, and there was a wide variety of both fiction and nonfiction. Schul might stop at eighth grade in his community, but many church members he knew were avid readers. He chose a book, and when he saw that Ruby still sat on the front porch, he walked out to join her.

"Thought you'd be gone by now."

She shrugged. "He's just running a little late."

"That's Isaiah."

"How did you know it's Isaiah?"

"Heard his stereo system when he brought you home last night."

Ruby winced. "I'm surprised the bishop hasn't had a word with him. I'm schur he knows about it, the way Isaiah plays it so loudly."

"I think the bishop may just be glad Isaiah didn't leave because he liked some aspects of Englisch life too much."

"Perhaps." She looked at the book in his hands. "I loved that book. Eli got me to read it years ago."

"Ya?" He looked at it.

She nodded. "We'll have to talk about it after you read it." Then she frowned. "Where are the Kinna?"

"My Mudder took them for a sleepover."

"Ah. I bet they'll enjoy that. I always loved coming here when I was a Kinner." She gazed out at the road, but it seemed it was more reflective than that she was looking for Isaiah. "It wasn't just that I got away from my family—not that I didn't love them, but it was nice to get some individual attention here. And Leah encouraged my interest in sewing quilts, and Eli told me he wanted me to read every book on the bookshelves."

"Wow. There's a lot of books in there."

She grinned. "I've read most of them. Leah keeps adding to them. I need to pick up some for her from the library this week. She's got some on hold, and the library called."

"I'm going into town on Thursday. We could go together."

He supposed he shouldn't have been surprised that she stared at him.

"Really?"

"Schur. I want to pick up a few books myself." He didn't want to tell her that one was a book on leukemia. He wanted to know more about Leah's condition.

"You can't get much time to read with the Kinna."

"I don't. Mostly I read before bed, after they're asleep."

The blare of music announced Isaiah's arrival.

"Well, I have to go. What time do you want to leave?"

"Maybe ten or eleven."

She nodded. "That works for me. See you. And enjoy the book."

He lifted a hand to Isaiah as they descended the porch steps. Then he took the turn to his house and climbed the steps to go inside. He'd enjoyed talking to Ruby and realized they hadn't once had heated words.

He turned to shut the door to his house, watched the buggy roll down the road, and felt a momentary stab of regret that she was going off with Isaiah. Well, there was always tomorrow. Maybe they could get on better footing, even if it was only for the sake of being around Leah.

CHAPTER ELEVEN

Ruby relaxed back against the seat in the buggy. She knew she shouldn't have worried when Isaiah was running late, but she had found herself getting a little nervous when the minutes ticked past.

So it had been a relief when he showed up and apologized for being late. He'd explained that he'd had to work and then run home to clean up and change.

The strong scent of aftershave drifted across the buggy. It was so strong that she thought her eyes would water. Aftershave wasn't something worn by the men she knew. She suspected it was something else, like the stereo system, he liked from his days of Rumschpringa.

"So how was your day?" Ruby asked. Isaiah had worked as a carpenter with his Dat since he graduated from Schul.

He shrugged. "Allrecht. We put in kitchen cabinets in an Englisch house." He glanced over at her. "You look pretty."

Her heart skipped a beat. She wasn't used to compliments from men. "Danki."

"How do you like living with your Aenti?"

"I like it. She's been doing fairly *gut* with her treatments."

"She has a nice farm."

Ruby nodded. "Takes a lot of work. Daniel helps Gideon some on it."

"Is she going to have to sell it now that she's sick?"

"What? Nee. It's her home. And she's going to get well."

"Schur." Once they were clear of the community, he reached for the dials on his stereo system. Soon loud rock was pouring out, and he was moving to the beat.

Conversation was impossible. Ruby opened her mouth to say something but didn't really know how to. He finally turned the "music" down when they approached the ice cream shop.

They got out and ordered and then sat at a picnic table under the shade of a big umbrella.

"You seem different lately," he said as he ate his banana split. "Since you moved in with Leah."

"Different *gut* or different bad?" She sipped her root beer float.

"Different *gut*." He gave her a flirtatious look.

She didn't know what to say, felt off-balance. He'd never directed his considerable charm at her in all the years she'd known him. "Danki," she said and stared down at the ice cream in the drink.

He began telling her about his day, complaining that his Dat was driving him hard. "Not sure carpentry's for me."

She scooped up the last of the ice cream in the drink. "What would you rather do?"

He shrugged. "Thought about farming maybe. Be my own boss."

"Land's expensive in Lancaster County. At least that's what my Dat said once. Farmland's being crowded out by development, homes being built."

"Ya. Pretty much you have to inherit." He finished his treat and stood. "Ready to go?"

She rose but didn't follow him when she saw that he left his empty dish and crumpled paper napkin on the table. Gathering it up, she carried it to the nearby garbage bin and tossed everything in.

He turned on the music as soon as he got into the buggy. Well, some men weren't great talkers, she told herself.

She gazed out at the passing scenery. Crops were growing well in the fields. Spring had been mild so far, with just the right amount of rain and no bad storms. She thought about what he'd said regarding wanting to be his own boss and possibly farming, and she realized that no farmer was really his own boss. Nature controlled everything.

Isaiah pulled up in front of Leah's house and turned the sound down. He gazed out at the house. "Big place," he said. "Eli and Leah never had Kinna."

"Nee."

"Guess it's *gut* you could quit your job to take care of her."

"It's what you do when it's Familye," she told him simply. "But it won't be for long, just until Leah finishes her treatment. And I'm sewing a quilt to put for sale in a shop in town." She smiled at him. "I had a nice time, Isaiah. Danki for the root beer float."

"Maybe we can do something the day after tomorrow."

"Schur."

"I'll pick you up about six. We'll have something to eat somewhere."

"Allrecht." She got out of the buggy and felt like she was floating as she went up the walk. It wasn't her first date ever, but it was a lot better than any she'd been on before. She climbed the porch steps and turned to wave goodbye at him, but the buggy was already rolling down the road.

The floating feeling didn't go away.

Isaiah stopped by to remind her of their date on his way home from work the next day—as if she could forget such a thing.

And when he showed up early for the date, she wasn't schur her feet actually touched the ground as she walked to his buggy.

"You look pretty," he said as she climbed into the buggy. "New dress?"

His compliment made her blush. "Danki. Ya, it's new."

Ruby knew Isaiah had dated many Maedels since they attended Schul together. Word got around, even though most singles kept dating quiet. She hadn't ever expected him to look her way and was still flattered by his attention.

Supper turned out to be subs he'd picked up on the way to her house. They took them to a park to eat. He apologized for not taking her to a fancy restaurant, saying he was running a little short of cash. Ruby didn't mind. She loved picnics. She'd have loved it more if he hadn't wanted to play his music loud again and they had talked more, but she'd have to think of a way to speak up. This dating thing was new to her.

As they drove home, he promised that after he got paid, they'd go to a fancy restaurant of her choice.

She didn't have any idea what that would be because she'd never been to one, so she said he'd have to choose. After she told him she'd had a *gut* time, they made plans for Friday.

And once again, she walked into Leah's house feeling as light as air.

Daniel picked Ruby up on Thursday, and they went into town together.

"I'm enjoying reading the book I borrowed from Leah," he told her.

"Great. I can't wait to hear what you think when you finish it."

He wondered if she discussed books with Isaiah when they went out but figured it wasn't his business. Isaiah didn't seem to be Ruby's type. Ruby was quiet, serious, and always ready to help others. Isaiah hadn't been interested in Schul, took life lightly, and had always been a charmer. Well, who knew why people were attracted to each other?

They stopped at the library and agreed to meet back at the checkout counter in an hour. Daniel consulted with a librarian, who found him a book on leukemia. Then he chose some classic fiction titles and a few books he thought his Kinna would like and just enjoyed the quiet time browsing because he seldom had such free time. A glance at the clock on the wall told him he needed to head for the checkout counter to meet Ruby.

He found her standing there, waiting for him. She'd chosen several books with quilt patterns, a cookbook, and a fiction title by the author he was reading. She added the books waiting for Leah and looked up with a smile when he approached. The smile faded when she saw the book about leukemia.

"I thought I'd do some research on it," he said quietly as they walked to the buggy and climbed inside. "I had some questions and didn't want to ask her."

She nodded. "I checked that book out right after she told us," she said quietly. "I had some concerns, but I didn't want her to feel I was prying or worried. She needs us to believe she's going to beat this."

"Leah's a strong woman. One of the strongest I've ever known."

Daniel stared ahead for a long moment, wondering if he was saying it more to convince himself or her. He turned to her. "Let's have lunch. We need to talk."

Daniel could tell he had surprised her. She glanced at him, startled, and her eyes were big and filled with doubt. He'd never noticed that they were the color of melted chocolate.

Finally, she nodded. "Allrecht."

He checked for traffic and pulled onto the road. They went to a small restaurant that was a favorite of both local Amish and

Englisch and were able to get a table quickly since they were early for lunch.

The restaurant was like many in the area, decorated with quilts and photographs of the local scenery. Amish favorites were featured on the menu, and Ruby doubted anyone left without having a dessert after having to walk past a huge glass-fronted case filled with pies and cakes.

"Mary's been doing a lot of cooking since you've been teaching her," he told her as they studied the menu. "Samuel's even become more interested, although it's still a struggle to get him to eat vegetables."

"Vegedabbles," she corrected him with a smile.

"I didn't like them much as a Bu either," he admitted, chuckling at her use of Samuel's word for vegetables. "That changed when I married. Sadie had a way of making them delicious."

Their server took their orders and brought their drinks. The restaurant began filling a few minutes later. People they knew stopped by their table to say hello and ask Ruby about Leah.

"It's nice that so many people care about Leah," Ruby said as she sipped her iced tea.

"I couldn't have gotten through losing Sadie if I hadn't had Leah for a friend as well as a neighbor," he told her.

"She's always been my favorite Aenti. One time when I was little, my Eldres came to pick me up after a sleepover at her house, and I cried. I didn't want to go home. My Mudder wasn't very happy with me."

"I'm glad you're staying with her. I was worried about her being alone while she went through treatment. I want us to get along for her sake if for no other reason."

She met his gaze directly. "I figured you were being friendly because you want me to teach Mary how to make my cinnamon rolls."

The server came with their lunches. Distracted by what Ruby had said, he only remembered to thank the woman when she remained standing at the side of the table to make schur the food was what they wanted.

"I was joking," Ruby said with a grin when he continued to stare at her instead of picking up his fork. "Did you think Mary wouldn't tell me you wanted her to learn how to make them?"

"I should know better than to think she could keep a secret."

"That's not the only one," she said, then gave him a mysterious smile.

Disconcerted, he stared at her. "What does that mean?"

"Just kidding," she said and took a bite of her chicken sandwich.

He concentrated on his hot meatloaf sandwich. "Anyway, just wanted to declare a truce if I needed to."

"No need."

He set down his fork. "I just worry that Leah might not tell us if . . ." He swallowed hard against the lump in his throat.

"If her treatment isn't working," she said, her voice almost a whisper.

"Ya."

"She's always been honest with me. I guess we have to trust that if she's not doing well, she'll tell us."

"You're right," he said with a sigh. After a moment, he picked up his fork and began eating again.

He'd wondered if they'd find it awkward talking over lunch but found it surprisingly easy. It turned out they'd read many of the same books, and that launched a discussion that lasted all through the meal. Daniel told her a funny story about Samuel's latest mischief as they enjoyed the restaurant's apple pie, which they agreed was the best selection. He couldn't help expressing the hope that Mary's baking skills would soon include her Mudder's strawberry rhubarb pie.

"Give her time," Ruby advised. "She's learning so fast."

Daniel liked how Ruby didn't chatter like so many Maedels. She didn't flirt, either, although who would after he'd been rude enough to tell her he wasn't interested in getting married.

It was only when he realized those Amish friends who'd stopped by the table when they came in were leaving that Daniel noted the time.

"Guess we should go get the supplies we need," he said regretfully.

"Let me pay. You drove us into town."

"Absolutely not." He snatched up the check the server had brought. "Maybe next time."

She smiled and nodded. "Next time."

CHAPTER TWELVE

Ruby sat on the front porch on Friday, waiting for Isaiah to pick her up, and thought about the day before when she'd had lunch in town with Daniel.

The lunch invitation had surprised her. Enjoying herself had been even more surprising. And then when he'd suggested that they should have lunch again . . . well, that had completely floored her.

She smoothed the skirt of her blue dress and thought about how strange—and wunderbaar—it felt having two men being nice to her, and it gave her an unaccustomed thrill.

Leah came out and sat in the rocking chair with a glass of lemonade.

"Isaiah late again?"

Ruby smiled. "If he was on time, he'd be early."

"True. As I remember, he was even late being born. I remember he came three weeks late." She held out her glass and offered Ruby some of her lemonade, but Ruby shook her head.

They sat there, rocking, enjoying the breeze, and Leah finished her lemonade. She yawned and shook her head. "I think I'll go read." She rose, bent to kiss Ruby's cheek, then went back into the house.

Ruby closed her eyes and sent up a prayer for Leah. Her eyes flew open when she heard a blast of music as Isaiah pulled up in front of the house. As she walked down the porch steps, she heard the singer wailing loudly about livin' on a prayer.

"Bon Jovi," he said as she got into the buggy. When she stared at him, confused, he explained that it was the name of the band.

"Aren't you worried about the bishop? You're not supposed to have a stereo system in your buggy."

He rolled his eyes. "You sound like my Mudder. He's not gonna say anything to me. He's still trying to get me baptized."

She wasn't happy at being told she sounded like his Mudder, but when he glanced over and told her she looked pretty, she smiled.

"You look nice too."

"Mamm told me I needed to put on my Sunday best," he noted as he pulled out onto the road. "Said they expected better than my everyday gear at the place we're going."

"You schur I'm dressed right for it?"

He nodded.

As they pulled into the lot of the fancy restaurant, Isaiah warned her that the food was expensive. But he told her to order what she wanted because he'd decided they deserved a treat. He and his Dat had completed a big job, and he'd been given a little bonus in his weekly check.

"That seems to have put you in a *gut* mood," she told him. "But it wasn't necessary to do this."

"You're worth it."

The restaurant was so different from the one she and Daniel had eaten in earlier in the week. She tried not to gawk as they approached the man in a formal black suit who stood stiffly behind an elaborately carved wooden pedestal. She'd never seen a tuxedo except in pictures in a magazine.

The man looked a little unhappy when Isaiah gave him his name. Apparently, they were late for their reservation. Isaiah apologized but didn't look all that sorry. Ruby figured he was used to people not being happy with him for being late.

There were satin drapes at the window and paintings of foreign places on the wall. The carpet was lush beneath her feet as they were led to their table. Englisch couples in fancy clothes and lots of jewelry sat at the tables they passed. They tried not to stare at an Amish couple in such a place, and in turn, she tried not to feel awkward and out of place when she realized they were the only Amish couple there.

The man seated her and then disconcerted her by draping a linen napkin over her lap before he left them with large leatherbound menus. "Andre will be with you momentarily," he announced before striding off.

"Nice, huh? I wanted to take you someplace special," he said with a warm smile.

Ruby nodded but felt uncomfortable about the money he was spending when she looked inside the folder and saw the prices on the menu. After studying it thoroughly, she chose the grilled chicken breast—the cheapest thing she could find. And she ordered regular water, not the fancy sparkling kind the server asked if she wanted when she saw what the price was for a glass of iced tea.

Isaiah ordered a steak, and as they ate their salads, he talked about the job he and his Dat had finished that had resulted in the extra money he was using to pay for their nice meal out. Ruby didn't understand some of the details about the carpentry but listened attentively.

She was grateful when he changed the subject and asked how Leah was doing as he cut into the steak.

Remembering how she and Daniel had talked about books the day before, she asked him what he'd read lately. He started laughing and nearly choked on the bite of steak he'd put into his mouth.

"A book?" he asked, staring at her. "I haven't read a book since we went to Schul. And barely did there when I had to."

Now that she thought about it, she remembered that.

She searched for something else to talk about.

"How's the farm doing?" he asked.

"The farm?"

"Ya, Leah's farm. Tell me what Gideon's planted, how the crops are doing."

She was surprised at the question, but he'd said he thought he'd like to farm when they talked recently. She hadn't been aware he was so interested, but he peppered her with more queries, and she didn't know how to answer them.

"I help Leah with the kitchen garden, but I don't have anything to do with the farm," she apologized. "Gideon handles it, and Daniel comes over and helps a lot."

"Why would Daniel help?"

"They're friends as well as neighbors. He and Leah's Mann were friends as well. I think Daniel looks out for her."

The questions stopped when the server wheeled over a cart filled with the fanciest desserts Ruby had ever seen. After laughing loudly over the name of the decadent-looking chocolate confection called *mousse*—"Moose?"—Isaiah chose it. When the server left, he told Ruby it was just pudding. Whipped pudding.

"You should have gotten something," he said as he ate it.

But Ruby just couldn't make herself order dessert. They were as expensive as a lunch at the restaurant she and Daniel had gone to. She loved sweets as much as anyone else, but she could have a cookie or a slice of cake when she got home. Every Amish home had baked goodies on hand.

Isaiah winced a little when the check arrived in a leather folder but drew out hundred-dollar bills and tucked them inside without a qualm.

Ruby felt slightly ill thinking about the cost as they got up to leave the elegant restaurant.

But when Isaiah held her hand while he took the long way home in the moonlight, she knew she'd always remember the night she'd been treated to such a special evening.

CHAPTER THIRTEEN

The next afternoon, Ruby was standing at the stove, waiting for the tea kettle to heat water, when there was a knock on the kitchen door. Then it opened, and Daniel stuck his head in.

"Where's Leah?" he whispered.

"In the living room," she whispered back.

When he gestured for her to come closer, she walked over to him, curious about his behavior.

"Leah's birthday is coming up," he told her in a low voice as he kept an eye out for her Aenti.

"I know."

"I want to get her something special from the Kinna and me. Will you go into town with me and help me choose something?"

"Why don't you take the Kinna?"

He gave her a look. "Neither of them can keep secrets, remember?"

"Ah, I do remember now." The tea kettle screeched, so she walked over to turn the flame off. "Let me fix this tea for Leah, and then I'll go with you."

Leah walked into the room. "Go with him where?"

"Into town for a few supplies," Daniel said quickly.

"Do you mind if I go with? I'd like to drop off some work I've done for the arts and crafts gallery."

Daniel and Ruby exchanged looks. He was the first to come up with an excuse. "Uh, I was going to ask if you would look out for the Kinna if I don't get back in time," he told her. "You know, when they come home from Schul."

"Oh, schur," she said as she looked from one to the other. "Schur." She gestured at the square wicker basket filled with her sketches that sat on the bench by the door. "Would you mind dropping these by the arts and crafts gallery? Anna is expecting them."

"We can do that," Daniel said as he hefted the basket under one arm. "Ruby, I'll go hitch up the buggy."

Ruby tried to act natural as she turned to Daniel and said she'd be right over as soon as she changed.

Leah took a seat at the table as Ruby poured a cup of hot water and set it before her. Ruby was conscious of Leah studying her as she put the box of tea bags on the table. Then she ran upstairs to change out of her everyday dress.

"Do you need anything from town?" she asked when she returned to the kitchen.

"I can't think of anything." Leah sipped her tea and eyed Ruby speculatively. "Nee, wait," she said, and she got up to get her purse. "I want you to stop by the quilt shop and get me some fabric. I'll call Lillian and tell her what I want."

"Allrecht. I'm sorry you can't go, but I'm schur Daniel's grateful you can be here if the Kinna come home before we do."

"Ya, I'm schur he is."

Ruby wondered if it was her imagination that Leah's lips quirked just a little at the corners. Uncertain, she backed toward the door. "See you later. Don't go starting supper. I'll cook when I get back."

"I won't cook. You two have a *gut* time."

Ruby grabbed her purse and nearly ran from the house. Daniel was waiting in his buggy in the driveway. "I feel so guilty," she muttered as she climbed into the buggy and tried to catch her breath. "I think she thinks we're going to town to have fun."

"Well, I hope we have some fun," he said as he pulled out onto the road and started for town.

"You know what I mean. I think she thinks we're . . . going out on a date or something."

He chuckled and shot her a look that had her tilting her head and studying him. "What? Why are you looking at me like that?"

"Sorry. You looked just like Samuel before he got up to mischief the night Leah and I went to supper at your house. He had that sly grin and gleam of mischief in his eyes."

He grinned. "Like Dat, like Sohn, eh?"

She chuckled and nodded.

"Well, we can't help what Leah thinks, but she knows you're seeing Isaiah, right? So maybe she won't think we're a pair."

Funny he should use that word, she thought as they rode toward town. It was the one that Mary had used when Leah had done her drawings of the worrywarts.

"So, what do you think you want to get her for her birthday?" she asked him.

"I'm hoping you can help me think of something. She always says she doesn't want a fuss about her birthday. But I think we should do it this year. She's not had it easy with her treatments."

"While you were getting the buggy, she told me she was going to call ahead to the quilt shop for a few things I could pick up for her. Maybe we'll see something there."

"That's a *gut* idea."

"Can we drop off Leah's work first? That way, we won't be leaving it in the buggy and have anything happen to it while we're shopping."

"Schur."

The fields they passed were lush and green. She waved to farmers they knew as they passed them working on the warm spring day.

"Isaiah asked me questions about the farm when we had supper out," she told him. "I was surprised at him being interested in farming."

"So he isn't happy working as a carpenter with his Dat?"

"I don't think so. Says he thinks being a farmer means he can be his own boss. I don't think he's considering how much of a farmer's life is out of his control. I mean, a farmer can't control the weather or the prices he'll get for his crops or—"

"How much work it involves."

Ruby nodded and relaxed against the seat. "Well, it's nice to take a drive and not have to listen to what he calls music. He calls some of it *head-banging*. I had to ask him to turn it down because it was giving me a headache." She frowned and chided herself for sharing that. It was becoming entirely too easy to talk to the man. "Sorry, I shouldn't be complaining about him."

"No problem."

"Let's see if we can come up with some ideas for Leah," she suggested brightly, and they tossed them around as they rode toward town.

Daniel parked behind the arts and crafts gallery so that they could drop off Leah's artwork.

Once inside, they looked around to see if there was anything suitable for her, then left her drawings for Anna.

"Let's try the quilt shop next," Ruby suggested. "Leah said she was calling ahead for some things she wanted, so maybe we'll get an idea for her birthday present."

"Sure, but I'll wait outside," he said as they walked.

"What is it with men and quilt shops?" she asked him, amused. "You won't be asked to make a quilt if you step inside one."

"No sense taking chances."

"Maybe we should try the hardware store," she told him as they approached the quilt shop. "I'm not afraid to go into a hardware store. I went there with my Dat several times when I was a Kinner."

"I came here once with my Mudder," he told her as he opened the door for her to precede him.

"Let me guess. You were very little."

He chuckled. "Ya."

They went inside, and Daniel looked around while Ruby went to the shop counter to talk with Lillian about what Leah wanted.

Lillian already had the order waiting, and Leah had arranged payment over the phone, so there was nothing for Ruby to do but watch the shopkeeper put everything in a bag for her.

"Wait!" she said, reaching for the folded square of fabric Lillian was about to tuck into the bag. "This looks familiar." She frowned. "Ya, I remember I had trouble deciding whether to buy this or the periwinkle fabric last time I was in." She checked the yardage slip pinned to it. "That looks like the amount to make a dress. I guess Leah's going to make herself a new dress."

Lillian just smiled, put the fabric into the bag, and handed it to her. She looked over at Daniel. "Hello, Daniel. Nice to see you. I don't believe you've visited since you were a Kinner."

He grinned. "You're right."

"We're going to browse. Leah has a birthday coming up, and we're looking for something special for her."

The woman tilted her head and looked thoughtful. "I think she has nearly everything I could suggest. And she bought a new quilt frame last year. I'll let you know if I think of anything."

"Danki."

"Tell Leah I hope to see her again soon."

"I will."

They didn't find anything, so they left the shop and continued down the sidewalk.

Then Ruby stopped abruptly. "I think I know what we should buy for Leah. Art supplies. She's doing more artwork since she's been ill."

"But what do we get?"

"Charlotte will know. Leah's shopped in her art supply store for years. Look, I've been saving up. We could pool our money and get something nice."

Schur enough, Charlotte had suggestions and gathered together a basketful of things she said Leah would enjoy and then added a book of illustrations by Leah's favorite artist.

Ruby picked up some things for Mary and Samuel as well since they liked to visit and draw with her sometimes.

"Well, that worked out," Daniel told Ruby as they left the shop.

"Let's get some candy too," she said. "I know what she loves."

They walked and talked, and finally, Daniel suggested lunch.

"This is the kind of place I love," she said, settling into a booth in the restaurant where they'd had their first lunch together. "I feel much more comfortable here than the fancy restaurant where Isaiah took me."

"Oh?"

She told him about how Isaiah had wanted to celebrate at the fancy restaurant and how the man she'd since learned was called a *maître d'* had seated her and placed a napkin on her lap.

"Then I took one look at the menu prices, and I was afraid to order anything. I ended up getting grilled chicken. It was the cheapest thing I could find on the menu. And no dessert."

"No dessert?"

She shook her head. "And I dearly love dessert. I always look to see what the dessert is on a menu at a new restaurant before I order my meal. I'd eat dessert first if I could," she admitted and blushed. "Sounds silly."

Daniel shook his head. "I love dessert. I'm thrilled Mary is learning to bake." He glanced at the dessert section of the menu, although he'd been here often enough to know pretty much all of what it offered. "They have strawberry rhubarb pie today. One of my favorites."

"Mine too."

"We have more in common than I realized," he said thoughtfully.

"We do?"

"Our church. We went to the same Schul—"

"Not at the same time."

"Nee. I'm older." The server came to take their orders. When she left, he continued, "We both love Leah. And Kinna. Where we live. This restaurant."

A server walked by with a tray of desserts for another table.

"And desserts," they said in unison and laughed.

Daniel liked the way her eyes sparkled when she laughed.

"They had weird things on the menu too," she told him. "Escargot—that's snails. Snails! And frog legs. I hope Samuel never goes there. Imagine if he found out that's what some people do with frogs."

"One of my *Onkels* took me out to catch frogs one day," he said, remembering. "I was about Samuel's age. It was great fun eating some of the gummy bears we were using for bait. But then I caught a frog and handed it to my Onkel. He held it up and said, 'Hmm, you caught a chunky monkey. Look at those plump legs. There's some good eating,' and he put it in an ice chest. I had no idea that's what we were going to do with them. I ran home."

"I'm so glad I'm a Maedel," she said, shaking her head. "That's one more thing I never did because I wasn't a Bu."

He chuckled. "Hope that story doesn't put you off your lunch."

"Nee. I'm too hungerich." But she looked for a change of subject in case he had more stories like that and ruined her appetite. "I guess you should take Leah's presents to your house and hide them," she said as she sipped her tea. "If I walk in with anything, she'll want to know what I bought."

"I agree. I'll put them where I hide Christmas presents from the Kinna."

"Where's that?"

He shook his head and grinned. "I don't know if I can trust you with that secret."

"I can keep secrets!"

"One of the Kinna could get it out of you," he said, enjoying teasing her. "Mary could. Look how she's talked you into teaching her how to bake a couple of times a week."

"Totally different. And I enjoy having her. She didn't have to talk me into it."

Their food came, and they began eating. He realized he was really enjoying spending time with Ruby and decided he wanted to know her better. "I think it's time you come to supper again," he said suddenly.

"You do?"

He nodded.

"You mean Leah and me?"

"The invitation is for you," he said, looking at her intently. "You can bring Leah if you want."

He could tell he'd taken her by surprise. "Think about it," he told her, pretending a casual air he found he didn't have. It was possible she was too interested in Isaiah to want to spend time with him.

Ruby took a sip of her tea and then nodded. "I'd love to come." She tilted her head and studied him. "Will Samuel be bringing his frog to supper?"

CHAPTER FOURTEEN

Ruby sat with Leah in the living room, working on their quilts. The day was rainy and cool, and it was a *gut* one to be inside.

She found herself daydreaming as she sewed. For the first time in her young life, she'd felt the unaccustomed sweetness of a man flirting with her when Isaiah took her to the elegant restaurant.

And Daniel had asked her to help him find a birthday present for Leah, and they'd spent hours together. Then he'd asked her to come to supper with him and his Kinna. He'd let her know the invitation could include Leah if she wanted, but it was really for her.

And he'd had this look in his eyes. . . . It had held interest in her and had warmed her heart but made her uncertain at the same time. Could he really be attracted to her?

"You're daydreaming again," Leah said, her tone amused.

"Hmm?" She looked up from the quilt.

"You've been someplace else since you got up."

"I'm sorry."

"I didn't say that to make you feel bad. I think I know what you're thinking of. Or should I say whom. I was a Maedel once. I remember what it felt like to have a young man pay attention to me." She sighed and set the quilt she was working on aside and looked off into the distance.

When she got that faraway look in her eyes, Ruby knew Leah was thinking of her beloved Eli.

Ruby was glad Leah couldn't see inside her mind and know she was thinking about Daniel and not Isaiah.

"So did you have a *gut* time with Daniel yesterday?"

Ruby felt herself coloring. How did she know she was thinking of him?

Leah chuckled. "That *gut*, eh?"

"We just did some shopping and had lunch." She concentrated on making tiny stitches in the quilt. Quilt buyers looked for things like that when they came to Lillian's shop.

"Sometimes it takes another man showing interest to make a man pay attention," she said sagely.

"Leah, stop playing matchmaker. Daniel and I are just friends." She knotted her thread, clipped it with scissors, and concentrated on threading her needle. "We're invited to supper tonight."

"Ya?"

She nodded. "Apparently, Mary is really enjoying cooking and wants us to come over."

"That'll be nice. Daniel's Kinna are so well behaved."

"Except when one of them isn't," Ruby said with a grin, remembering Samuel's prank. "I asked Daniel if Samuel would be inviting his frog."

"Samuel was so disappointed you didn't flinch at it jumping onto your plate," Leah said, chuckling. "I'm ready for lunch. Are you?"

"Ya." She set aside the quilt and followed Leah into the kitchen.

A big pot of chicken and corn soup with *Rivels* had been simmering since they got up this morning, filling the kitchen with its rich scent. Ruby loved the soup, with its little dumplings and noodles.

By the time Leah finished the hearty soup, she seemed to be ready to nod off. "Rainy days make me sleepy," she confessed, then shook her head.

Ruby had never known the woman to be anything but a barrel of energy no matter what the weather.

"It's a *gut* day for a nap," she agreed. "Why don't you go lie down for a little while?"

Leah yawned. "I think I will. But don't let me sleep too long, or I'll have trouble sleeping tonight."

"I won't." She watched Leah climb the stairs slowly and felt tears rush into her eyes. Determined not to cry, she blinked hard at them and rose to wash the dishes. But the tears slipped down her cheeks and fell into the dishwater. When she heard the door open, she grabbed the corner of her apron and wiped them away.

"Ruby! What's wrong?" Daniel asked as he walked into the room.

She shook her head and didn't turn. "Nothing."

"You're crying." He moved closer. "Is it Leah? Is she feeling worse?"

Ruby heard the worry in his voice. She turned. "She's just very tired today and went upstairs for a nap. But you know Leah. She's always been a barrel of energy."

"Some of her tiredness may be age," he said in a reassuring tone. "We shouldn't think it's all because of her treatments."

"I know." She sighed. "Did you come over to talk to her?"

"Nee. To you. I just wanted to make schur you were coming to supper tonight. Mary asked me at breakfast if I'd asked you. I told her yes."

"I'll be there. I invited Leah too."

"That's fine. I'd feel better if she wasn't alone now anyway. Well, I'll get back to work. See you at five thirty." He paused at the door. "Ruby, remember that Leah's a strong woman."

She nodded. "You've said that before."

"Believe it." He looked at her for a long moment. "Do you want me to stay?" he asked quietly.

"Nee. I'm fine."

He hesitated and then, after a brief nod, left her. She watched him walk out to talk to Gideon in the fields before he headed to his own farm. Before he left Leah's property, he glanced in her direction. Embarrassed to be caught watching him, she looked down at the dishwater until she was schur he was gone.

After she finished cleaning up the kitchen, she went back to sewing the quilt. She was making *gut* progress and hoped the work would go quickly. She wanted to give most of the money she earned to her Eldres to help them since she was no longer working a job and giving them her paycheck.

And maybe buy fabric to make just one more new dress. . . .

She glanced at the clock and decided it was time to wake Leah. Before she went upstairs, she filled the tea kettle and set it on the stove to heat.

But when she tapped on the doorjamb, she saw Leah was already awake and sitting on the side of her bed. She looked pale and shaken.

"I've been sitting here for five minutes," she said, jerking her head at the battery-operated clock next to her bed. "I can't drum up the energy to stand."

"There'd be nothing wrong with you resting some more."

"Nee. What if I never got up again?"

Ruby shoved down her own fear and made a tsking sound. "You? Not likely. Why don't we go downstairs, have a cup of tea, and see how you feel? We can call the doctor if you want. I'm schur this is just a temporary thing." She prayed silently that it was. "Komm—I'll help you."

Leah sighed. "I'll let you."

They went down the stairs carefully, with Leah holding the banister and Ruby's arm around her waist.

The tea kettle was screeching when they reached the kitchen. After she settled Leah in a chair at the table, Ruby fixed them tea and put a plate of cookies in front of her.

"Maybe a little sugar will give you some energy."

Ruby glanced at the kitchen clock. They were due at Daniel's in an hour. There was still time for Leah to feel better. Otherwise, she was going to have to tell him they couldn't make it. She wasn't leaving Leah alone.

Daniel thought inviting Ruby to supper was inspired. Ya, Mary had suggested it, but it worked out well because he was becoming interested in getting to know Ruby better.

He hadn't been ready to look for a new Fraa yet, and whenever the bishop suggested he should, Daniel had wondered how the man thought a single Eldre could manage it. Where would he find time to date when he had a farm and two Kinna to care for? His Mudder had offered to babysit, but he hated to ask her with all she had to do.

He and Ruby knew each other from church and living in the same small community. But she was younger than him, and they hadn't attended Schul at the same time and done things together like he and Sadie had. And he knew he'd resisted getting to know her better because Leah had been less than subtle about trying to interest him in Ruby.

"They're late," Mary said.

Daniel glanced at the clock on the wall. "Just a few minutes."

Mary put her hands on her hips and frowned at him. "We need to eat while it's hot."

He bit the inside of his mouth to keep from grinning. How often had he called her and Samuel to supper in the past? he wondered.

"I'm hungerich," Samuel complained.

"You're always hungerich," Daniel pointed out. The Kinner was growing like a weed. Daniel remembered how much he'd eaten growing up. His Dat had said he had a hollow leg.

"Go see if they're coming," Mary said. "Please."

"Fine. But only if you sit at the table and don't go near the stove while I'm gone."

"Hurry. The biscuits have to come out soon," she told him, eyeing the oven timer.

So he went next door and found Ruby standing on the back porch. Leah sat in one of the rocking chairs with her arms folded across her chest. He didn't like how pale she looked—how out of breath she seemed.

"Something wrong?" he asked, sensing an air of tension between them.

"I'm fine," Leah said quickly, shooting Ruby a mutinous look. "Just need to catch my breath."

"Allrecht," he said easily. "No rush."

"She's been feeling weak since she took a nap," Ruby explained. "But she wouldn't let me cancel supper at your house."

"It's just a temporary weakness," Leah insisted. "If I feel worse, I assure you I'll go back to bed."

"Well, we can do one of two things," he told them. "We can bring supper over here—"

"We are *not* going to that trouble," Leah said.

"Or I can escort you there." He held out his arm to her.

"Such a fuss," she complained. But she got to her feet and took his arm.

"Ruby, would you mind going ahead to see that Mary doesn't get the biscuits out of the oven by herself? She was watching the timer when I left."

"Schur." She hurried ahead.

When Daniel and Leah walked into the kitchen, he saw that Ruby was pulling the pan of biscuits from the oven as Mary watched.

"They look wunderbaar," she told Mary. "Light and flaky and just the right golden-brown color. Your Mudder would be so proud of you."

Mary beamed. "It's like you said. Ovens are different. I have to leave them in about three minutes longer than you do in your oven."

"Practice makes perfect."

"When are we going to eat?" Samuel asked. He sat, head on his hand, elbow on the table, and pouted. "I've been hungerich forever."

Daniel escorted Leah to a chair, and when she was seated, he picked up the paper napkin at her plate and spread it across her lap in an exaggerated fashion.

"Why, Daniel, what's this about?" Leah asked, chuckling.

"I hear that's what they do at the elegant restaurants," he told her and winked at Ruby.

"Really? I wouldn't know."

Ruby helped Mary carry the platter of pot roast and vegetables to the table and didn't say anything. But he saw her trying to hide a grin.

Daniel caught Ruby watching Leah during supper. She looked relieved as her Aenti grew more animated and ate more than she usually did. Finally, Ruby appeared to relax, and she chatted easily with Mary about her cooking and drew Samuel out by asking about his frog.

Then he realized Leah was watching him watching Ruby. She raised her eyebrows, and there was a knowing look in her faded blue eyes. He nodded and she smiled, and if there was a trace of smugness in it, he found he didn't mind.

Eli had once told him that Leah was always right.

Well, he was willing to admit she might be right that Ruby was a wunderbaar young Maedel.

He'd thought by having Ruby over for supper, he'd have a chance to get to know her a little better. But Mary chattered about cooking, and Samuel spilled his milk, and before he knew it, everyone was scraping their plates clean.

Daniel and Samuel helped clear the plates, and as he did, Daniel found himself wondering how interested Ruby was in Isaiah, who schur didn't have any problems finding the time to take her out without doing so during Schul hours like he had to. On the other hand, Daniel liked that Ruby didn't appear to be impressed that Isaiah had taken her someplace so fancy. She really looked like she was enjoying the simple supper with his Familye.

Ruby smiled at Mary when she proudly set a big bowl of banana pudding studded with slices of banana and vanilla wafers on the table for dessert.

"Now that's dessert!" she said, earning a smile from his Dochder.

And from him.

CHAPTER FIFTEEN

"It's been too long since we had a Schweschder Day," Miriam told Leah as she walked into the kitchen one afternoon.

She set a basket of vegetables on the kitchen counter, took off her bonnet, and hung it on a peg by the door. "You schur you feel up to us making a big batch of soup?"

"Your Dochder doesn't let me overdo it," Leah told her. "I can certainly sit here at the table and chop vegetables. It won't be like other Schweschder Days where we planted a kitchen garden together or cleaned someone's house for them or went shopping. But this'll be fun."

Ruby just smiled and ignored the comment about not letting Leah overdo it as she washed the vegetables. She put them in a colander she set on the table in front of Leah. "Having jars of homemade soup will be wilkumm this winter."

Three dozen jars were already washed and sat on the counter, ready for the finished product. She walked over to the stove, where two big pots of beef and soup bones simmered in broth.

"Emma will be along soon," Miriam told them as she got a wooden chopping board and a sharp knife and sat at the table.

"Is she bringing my favorite Bu?" Ruby asked her.

"Why would she bring Daniel?" Leah asked with a grin.

Ruby rolled her eyes.

Emma arrived minutes later carrying her Boppli, Aaron. She looked flushed and a little stressed.

"You're late," Ruby said.

"I know. At the last minute, Aaron spit up on his clothes. I had to change him."

Ruby held out her arms, and Aaron chortled and went into them. He was a chubby-cheeked Boppli with downy blond hair and big blue eyes and had such a calm, sweet nature.

"Can you watch him for a little while for me?" she asked Ruby. "I need to run an errand in town."

"Of course." She bounced Aaron on her hip. "I was just saying he's my favorite Bu!"

Aaron let out a high-pitched cry of delight and enthusiastically patted Ruby's cheeks. She looked at Emma with wide eyes as she registered his weight. "Oh my, he feels like he's gained weight since I held him two weeks ago. He's growing so fast!"

"I know." She took the diaper bag she carried and set it on the bench near the back door. "I know the three of you are busy making soup today. Are you schur you don't mind?"

"I'm happy to do it."

Emma kissed her Sohn's cheek. "I'll be back soon. Be *gut* for your Aenti Ruby." She frowned at him for a moment, then looked at Ruby. "Hope he isn't fussy for you. I think he's got another tooth coming in. I put his teething ring and the ointment for his gums in the diaper bag."

"Don't worry, Mamm. He'll be fine."

Ruby tilted her head and studied her Schweschder. Pregnancy suited her. She glowed as she had for some time and looked so happy. Ruby was glad things were going well with the pregnancy since Emma and her Mann wanted a big Familye.

"Aaron can help us cut up vegetables," she told Emma.

"Very funny," Emma said. She bent to kiss her Mudder and Leah on the cheek and then rushed out the door.

Aaron gurgled, and Ruby turned her attention to him. "So, say hello to Leah."

Leah put down her knife and wiped her hands on a dish towel. "Let me have him."

Aaron held out his arms and went into Leah's. Ruby watched Leah embrace him.

"Oh, it's so *gut* to hold a Kinner," she said. "It's been so long since there's been a little one in this house. Maybe we won't give him back."

But after a few minutes, Leah handed him to Ruby. "Takes more energy than I remember being with a Boppli," she confessed. "That's why God gives *Bopplin* to the young."

They didn't have a high chair, so Ruby sat Aaron on a chair and tied an apron around his waist to hold him in place while they prepared the vegetables. He took it with his usual good nature and watched them avidly.

"Well, I'm feeling more tired than I thought," Leah admitted. "I think I'll go lie down for a few minutes if you two don't mind."

"Of course we don't," Miriam said. "You're schur you're allrecht?"

"Just fine. See you in a little while."

Ruby saw Aaron yawn. "He'll be taking one soon as well, from the looks of him."

Miriam waited until Leah had climbed the stairs. "Is she really allrecht?"

Ruby nodded. "She was up early. Try not to worry, Mamm. Leah is going to be here to enjoy the soup when fall comes."

Aaron began rubbing a fist over his mouth and whimpering.

"What's the matter, dear one?" she asked him. "Is your tooth bothering you?" She pulled the teething ring out of the bag and let him chew on it. When he continued to fuss, she decided to take him out of the improvised high chair. "I think I'll take him out to the front porch and rock him."

"*Gut* idea. I'll finish the soup."

Ruby took Aaron out to the porch and sat in the rocking chair, setting it in motion with her foot. He chewed on the teething ring. "Let's just try this, and maybe you'll fall asleep and you won't feel that tooth bothering you," she soothed.

But when he continued to whimper, she wished she'd brought the tube of ointment out with her.

"Got a visitor there, eh?"

Ruby looked up and saw Daniel standing at the foot of the porch stairs. "I'm watching him while Emma's gone to town. She said he's teething. I was just about to go in and get the ointment she's using on his gums."

Daniel climbed the stairs and held out his arms. "Let me hold him while you get it and put it on him."

She handed him over. "Danki."

While she was rooting around in the diaper bag for the tube of ointment, she heard something crash upstairs. She dropped the tube and raced up the stairs to Leah's bedroom.

When she got to the door, she saw Leah kneeling on the floor, picking up shards of glass.

"Let me do that!" she cried and rushed over to help Leah stand.

"It slipped out of my fingers," Leah said.

Ruby bent to pick up the pieces, and that's when she saw there was blood on them. She looked at Leah and saw her sitting on the bed, dabbing at her hand with a tissue.

"I'll get a bandage," Ruby told her as she stood.

"It's nothing. Don't fuss."

"We don't want it to get infected. Remember, your immune system is down." She cleaned and bandaged the cut on Leah's finger, picked up the broken pieces of glass, then returned to the front porch.

When she walked out, full of apologies, the tube of ointment in her hand, Daniel looked up and held a finger to his lips. Aaron lay sleeping in his arms.

Ruby tiptoed over to Daniel. "I'm so sorry," she whispered. "Leah needed me." She told him what had happened.

"No worries," he said easily as he looked down at Aaron. "I was just remembering holding my Kinna when they were this age. Sometimes it feels like it was just yesterday."

Daniel looked up at her. "If Aaron is still here when Mary comes home from Schul, I'll get asked when we can have another Boppli. I don't think she'd even mind if it was another Bruder, to tell you the truth."

"Even if he is a mischief-maker like Samuel?"

He chuckled. "I don't think she's thought that far ahead. She'd just like a Boppli." *And a Mudder*, he thought, but he didn't say so.

"I can take Aaron now if you need to go back to work."

"I have some time. Sit. Seems you've got double duty today, caring for a Boppli and Leah."

"Neither of them is any trouble."

She sat, and they rocked companionably without speaking. Daniel liked how she could be such *gut*, quiet company.

The scents of rich earth, of growing crops, of the flowers Leah loved planted in the front garden reached him on the warm breeze. It was moments like this that made all the hard work of a farm worth it.

And when he glanced down as Aaron moved in his sleep and smiled, he yearned for more. He and Sadie had hoped to have a big Familye. . . .

Daniel found himself looking up at Ruby and caught her looking at him. Their gazes locked, and something passed between them.

She was the first to speak. "I made some lemonade. Would you like a glass before you go back to work?"

"That'd be nice."

Relieved—and not sure why—he shook his head as she went into the house. When she returned with two tall glasses of icy lemonade, he felt more like himself. He took the glass she offered with his free hand and drank it in a couple of long gulps, then set it down on the nearby table.

"Well, guess I'd better get back to work," he told her regretfully. "This has been nice."

She stood and bent to lift Aaron from his arms, and as they exchanged the precious bundle, his hand brushed her arm, and his gaze flew to hers. Her rich brown eyes looked like dark chocolate as they widened at the contact, and then, blushing, she looked down at the Boppli and stepped away.

"Danki for the help," she told him, avoiding his gaze as she took her seat and gently rocked the still-sleeping Kinner.

"You're wilkumm," he said, hearing the gruffness in his voice. "Danki for the lemonade."

"Oh, I never asked you. Did you come over to see Leah?"

"Nee. I saw you when I came out to the front yard to check the mail. Thought I'd say hello." He got to his feet and headed for the stairs. "See you later."

He returned to his fields and walked through them, checking on growth, checking on any pests in his corn crop. The green leaves rising from the rich earth looked healthy and showed no sign of anything concerning. He heard a rumble, and when he glanced up, he saw clouds forming. An afternoon rain would be welcome.

The days were getting warmer and warmer. Spring was a short season in Lancaster County. Summer, with its hot days, though, always seemed to stretch on forever.

Farming and parenting had so much in common, he mused as the sun beat down on his shoulders. You nurtured and worried over Kinna and crops. Took the *gut* with the not-so-*gut* with your partner and God.

And when you didn't have a partner to walk with, you got through it somehow, with God always at your side.

He stopped, took off his straw hat, and wiped the sweat from his brow, then settled the hat on his head again. As he did, he glanced over at Leah's house. He could tell from the direction of the sun that it was almost time for his Kinna to come home. Would Emma's Boppli still be at Leah's? If Mary wanted to go over for a baking lesson, he'd have to tell her that it wasn't a *gut* day—that Ruby had her hands full watching Aaron.

And then Mary would surely want to go see the Boppli.

He sighed and shook his head as he began walking again, thinking how hard it was for Kinna to understand God's timing when he didn't understand it himself. Yesterday evening, he'd invited Ruby over to supper to get to know her better, but he hadn't really had a chance to talk to her much with the Kinna and Leah there. It was time for a different plan.

"Daed! We're home!" Samuel shouted from the edge of the field.

"So I hear," he called back. And so did everyone for a mile on each side of them, he thought with a grin. Samuel had never been a quiet Bu.

He walked back to the house and went inside with Samuel. Mary was already there, cleaning out the lunch boxes both had taken to Schul and washing the thermoses they'd had filled with milk. When she finished, he washed his hands and fixed them a snack of apples and cheese cubes, then listened to them chatter about their day while he drank a glass of iced tea.

"May I go see Ruby and have a baking lesson?" Mary asked.

"She's busy today," he told her.

"Doing what? Is Leah sick?"

Confronted with a direct question, he had to give her an honest answer. "She's taking care of Emma's Boppli."

Her eyes shone. "I want to go say hello. Please, can I say hello?"

He sighed. "I don't want you to bother her. Aaron was fussy earlier. He's teething."

"*You* got to see him."

That he had. He sighed and nodded. "Five minutes. And if she's busy, you come straight home."

"I will."

Samuel just sat at the table while Mary rushed out the door, then popped another cheese cube into his mouth.

"You don't want to see the Boppli?"

"Nee. Can I have a cookie?"

Daniel stared at him.

"May I have a cookie?"

"One."

Daniel got up and looked at the menu Mary had posted on the refrigerator. Tonight was ham-salad sandwiches. That would be *gut* after a warm day in the fields, he thought.

"Daed?"

"Hmm?" He turned away from the refrigerator.

"Where do Bopplin come from?"

He froze and cast about for what he'd told Mary when she had asked several years ago.

There was a knock on the door, and Gabriel poked his head in. "Got a minute?"

"Schur." He turned to his Sohn, who was sliding out of his chair.

"Can I go play at Ike's house?" Samuel asked.

"An hour," Daniel told him, feeling relieved. "Ask his Mudder if it's allrecht with her, and make schur you come back in an hour."

Gabriel's question about whether Daniel had heard anything about a fellow farmer needing some help was a lot easier to answer than Samuel's would have been.

Daniel settled down with a cup of coffee after he finally got the Kinna to bed.

Mary had talked and talked about how adorable Aaron was and how *gut* Ruby was with him. And she chattered about going to Leah's the next day to learn how to bake with Ruby as she packed lunches for herself and Samuel. Finally, she'd worn down and gone upstairs. Samuel had been subdued and settled down with a book in bed. Daniel missed his asking for a bedtime story, but it had been months since he'd done that.

Both his Kinna were growing up too soon.

As he drank his coffee, he tried not to remember how this had always been his favorite time of the day, when he and Sadie would talk, just the two of them, before going up to bed. Now the only sound was the clock on the wall ticking off the time.

He found himself remembering that moment of awareness he'd had when he accidentally touched Ruby's arm that afternoon, and he'd seen it in her eyes as well. It was the first time he'd felt any kind of reaction to a woman since Sadie. He'd been able to push aside thinking about it while he was busy with chores and the Kinna, and knew he couldn't think about it now, or he'd feel even lonelier than he did some nights.

With a sigh, he did his nightly check that the doors were locked and headed up to bed.

CHAPTER SIXTEEN

Ruby pulled the pan of chocolate chip cookies from the oven, set it on the stove, and used a spatula to transfer the cookies to a cooling rack. As she did so, she saw Samuel start for the back door.

"Don't you want one?" she asked. He was usually first in line for cookies when they baked them.

"Nee, Danki," he said.

She thought that was odd since he'd helped her and Mary mix the ingredients. Shrugging, she picked one up and handed it to Mary. "Careful, they're hot." After she chose one for herself, she blew on it before she took a bite. She immediately knew something was wrong. The cookies were salty instead of sweet.

"Ugh," Mary said. "Ruby, they taste awful!" She walked over to the kitchen wastepaper basket to spit out the bite she'd taken.

"I'm afraid you're right." She followed Mary to spit hers out and tossed the rest of the cookie away. "I wonder what went wrong." She used a spoon to dip into the remaining dough in the bowl, tasted it, and found it salty. Frowning, she tried the ceramic canister of flour, then the sugar. "Ah, this is the problem. There's salt in the sugar canister."

Samuel had brought the canister to the counter.

She opened the back door. "Samuel?"

He'd been walking over to his house, but at the sound of her voice, he took off.

"Samuel Fisher! Komm here, please!"

He skidded to a halt and turned to face her. "What?"

"Did you do something to the cookies?"

Ruby saw him smirk before he carefully schooled his expression and shook his head. "I can't help it if they don't taste *gut*."

She hadn't said there was something wrong with the taste. "Samuel! That wasn't nice! You komm apologize to your Schweschder."

"You're not my Mamm!" he retorted. "You can't tell me what to do!" He ran off down the driveway.

Frowning, Ruby turned to go back inside, and just as she did, she heard the screech of brakes. She flew down the porch steps, her heart pounding, and ran down the driveway to the front yard. A car sat in the middle of the road, its door open. A man stood in front of the car, staring down at the road with a horrified expression.

"What happened?" she cried as she ran to him.

Then she saw Samuel lying in a crumpled heap at his feet. Ruby dropped to her knees beside him and touched shaking fingers to his chest. It rose and fell under them.

"He just ran into the road! I couldn't stop in time!"

She turned to see Mary running down the drive.

"Get your Dat!" she called to her. "Tell him Samuel's hurt!"

Mary turned and raced back to her house.

"I'll call 911," the man said as he pulled out his cell phone, then began talking rapidly to the dispatcher. "They want to know if he's breathing."

"Yes." *Thank You, God*, she thought.

He handed the phone to her. "Here, you talk to them. You tell them what they need to know about your son."

Ruby didn't bother to tell him Samuel wasn't her son. It wasn't important right now. She answered the dispatcher's questions as best as she could and was told paramedics were on the way.

Daniel came running down to them and knelt on the other side of Samuel.

"I'm sorry! I'm so sorry!" the man kept saying, his voice shaking. "Where is the ambulance? It should be here by now!"

"Has he woken up at all?" Daniel asked Ruby as he smoothed the hair back from Samuel's forehead.

She shook her head.

"I've got a blanket in my car," the man said. "I'll get it."

He handed it to Ruby, and she spread it over Samuel.

Samuel stirred and opened his eyes. "Daed?"

"Right here, Sohn."

"I hurt."

"I know. Lie still. We're going to take you to the hospital. They'll fix you right up."

"Is he gonna be allrecht, Daed?" Mary asked tearfully as she stood on the lawn next to the road.

Ruby rose and went to hug her. "He'll be fine."

Sirens blared as emergency vehicles pulled up, and things soon got chaotic. Ruby kept her arm around Mary as paramedics unloaded equipment and began working on Samuel. A police officer arrived, parked his car, and directed traffic as cars and buggies slowed to see what was happening.

It seemed to Ruby that it took a long time to put a neck brace on Samuel, slide a board underneath his body and one arm, and load him onto a gurney.

"I have to go with him to the hospital," Daniel said, looking worried as the gurney was lifted into the ambulance.

"Mary can stay with me," Ruby told him. "You call when you're ready to bring him home, and I'll come get you."

Daniel ran a hand through his hair and then settled his hat back on his head. "Danki. It might be a while." He handed her his cell phone. "Take this."

"But you might need it at the hospital."

He shook his head. "If I need to call you, I can use a hospital phone. This'll keep you from needing to run out to the phone shanty."

She nodded and took it. "Allrecht. We'll pray for Samuel."

He gave Mary a quick hug and then climbed into the ambulance. The doors snapped shut, and then the ambulance began racing to the hospital, siren blaring.

When Mary began to cry, Ruby patted her shoulder. "I bet Samuel's going to find it exciting to be riding in an ambulance," she told her, trying to sound cheerful.

The man who'd hit Samuel came over to apologize again. He looked near tears as he handed her the straw hat Samuel had been wearing. Its crown had been sliced open, and part of the brim was missing. She took it and tried to reassure him the accident hadn't been his fault, but he walked away shaking his head.

The police officer had some questions for Ruby. She answered them, and then she had one for him. "He won't be charged, will he? The man who hit Samuel? It wasn't his fault. Samuel ran into the road."

The officer shook his head. "No, he won't be charged. I'm sorry Samuel got hurt. Kids just don't think, do they?"

He left her his card, and finally, Ruby was able to lead Mary into Leah's house.

"Let's have a cup of tea," she said as they walked into the kitchen. "Or I could make you a cup of hot chocolate. Would you like hot chocolate?"

Mary nodded.

Leah came down the steps from the upstairs bedrooms, looking sleepy. "Did I hear a siren?"

Ruby told her what had happened as she filled the tea kettle and set it on the stove, starting with how Samuel had put salt in the sugar canister and ended up being hit by a car out in front of the house.

She felt a pang of guilt as she dumped the cookie dough into the trash can. "I shouldn't have scolded Samuel for his prank. Then he wouldn't have run in front of the car. . . ." She stopped, pressing her fingers to her trembling lips.

"You can't blame yourself," Leah said, then hugged her.

"Samuel shouldn't do bad stuff," Mary agreed as she sniffled and used a paper napkin to wipe her nose.

"Mary, could you go outside and see if Gideon is still in the fields?" Leah asked. "I need to ask him to do your Dat's evening chores for him."

"Daed's not coming home tonight?" Mary started to tear up again.

"I'm schur he will, but it might be late. You can sleep here until he gets home."

Ruby watched Mary leave and then turned to Leah. "I don't think Samuel likes me."

"Now, don't go saying that. He's always loved getting into mischief."

Ruby shook her head. "I wonder if he thinks his Dat is interested in me, and he doesn't want that."

Leah got out mugs and tea bags and set them on the table. "Even if that's true, he'll have to get over it. It's his Dat's decision."

"Well, if a man has Kinna, he should choose someone they love who also loves them."

"I love you," Mary said quietly.

Startled, Ruby turned and saw she'd come in and stood by the back door. "Danki, Mary. And I love you."

Mary ran to her and threw her arms around Ruby's waist. "I want Samuel to be allrecht. He can be a brat, but he's my Bruder. He's got to be allrecht."

"He will be," Ruby promised. And she hoped she wasn't promising something that wouldn't be true.

"Gideon wasn't in the fields," Mary told her.

"No problem. You and I can feed and water your horses when it's time."

"We need to pray for Samuel," Leah said. "Komm—let's sit and pray."

Daniel found it hard to stay calm like he knew he had to be for Samuel on the ride to the hospital. Hearing the siren, watching Samuel being hooked up to monitors, and seeing the concentration on the faces of the paramedics was nerve-racking.

"I know it looks scary," one of them said quietly when he saw Daniel watching them. "But it sounds like he was only unconscious for a few minutes, and his vitals look good. I just spoke to the hospital. They have a team waiting for us."

The ride seemed to take forever, but Daniel knew it was a matter of minutes. The paramedic had been telling the truth about a team waiting for Samuel at the hospital's emergency entrance. He was rushed into a cubicle inside, and a doctor and several nurses immediately began to work on him.

"I need to get some information from you," a nurse said, then led him into an adjoining space where he could still see Daniel through a window.

"I don't have insurance," he began, but the nurse shook her head.

"We know," she said patiently. "We're not worried about the bill. Your community has always settled up with us. I need Samuel's medical history."

Samuel had gotten into a lot of mischief but had never gotten hurt or been sick other than last year, when he'd had the flu that was going around. She jotted down what Daniel told her, and he thought she went still when she asked about Samuel's mother and he told her she was dead.

"So it's his first time to be in an emergency room," she said, meeting his gaze. "You're lucky. One of my boys manages to land in here at least once a year with broken bones, scrapes, something to give me gray hair."

"Can I go in and be with him?"

"It's best if we let them do what they need to, give them the room to work," she said. "They'll be taking him down for a CAT scan in a few minutes. Let me show you where the waiting room is."

Daniel felt like his feet were rooted in concrete. He just couldn't make himself move away from where he could watch what was going on. Somehow, he felt that if he could see what was happening, everything would be allrecht.

"Mr. Fisher? I assure you, your son's in excellent hands," she told him quietly. "I'll come for you as soon as you can see him."

He sighed and nodded. Before he could move, he saw the gurney with Samuel on it being pushed out of the room and down the hallway. A young nurse was talking to him as she pushed it.

The waiting room was empty. He sank into a plastic chair and felt helpless. Then he remembered how Ruby had said she and Mary would pray for Samuel. So he closed his eyes and prayed hard—as hard as he'd done when the police officer had come to his door to tell him that Sadie had been hurt in an accident in their buggy and he would take him to the hospital.

Then, he'd been too late. Sadie was gone before they got there.

He prayed harder, and when he opened his eyes, he saw the nurse who'd taken Samuel's medical history standing in the doorway.

"Things are looking good," she said with a gentle smile. "You can come with me. The doctor's ready to talk to you."

His legs felt weak when he stood, but he forced himself to walk to her.

"I thought your name was familiar when we talked earlier," she told him. "I was on duty the afternoon your wife was brought in. I want you to know we did everything we could to save her."

He nodded. "I know. Things don't usually go well when an automobile hits a buggy. I'm just glad she didn't take the Kinna with her that day. I might have lost all of them."

"Well, I think you're going to take Samuel home soon," she told him as she showed him into the cubicle.

Samuel looked so small on the gurney. But he was alert and talking to the doctor as Daniel went to his side.

"I got a broke-in arm," he said. "I'm getting a cast."

The doctor put up the X-ray, showed Daniel the break, and explained that Samuel would need surgery to set it. "We don't see any sign of a concussion, so we can proceed with surgery to set the arm. The surgery is a simple procedure and shouldn't take long."

No concussion. The news was better than he'd thought he'd get. He'd have liked it if surgery hadn't been needed to set the arm, but Daniel felt that was better than a concussion. He thanked the doctor.

Samuel was disappointed he wasn't going home immediately and anxious about surgery, but he calmed when Daniel explained that he'd be given something to help him sleep so that it wouldn't hurt when the arm was set.

"Are you going to be with me?" he asked.

"I can't be in the operating room, but I'll be right outside in a waiting room."

"Then we can go home?"

"We'll see." The doctor hadn't said when they could go home, so Daniel didn't want to promise anything.

"You won't leave without me?"

"Absolutely not."

Soon, Samuel was given a sedative and wheeled out for surgery. Daniel was allowed to walk with him, and then, after he kissed his Sohn's cheek, he had to watch the doors close.

With a sigh, he walked to the waiting room and found it occupied by several Eldres who looked up anxiously—obviously expecting to see a doctor or nurse—when he appeared in the doorway. He sat but found he was too restless, so he got up to walk up and down the hall.

Finally, his restless energy drained away. He returned to the waiting room, which had emptied. He used the phone there to call Ruby and tell her that Samuel didn't have a concussion.

"Oh, that's so *gut* to hear."

"But he had to have surgery to set the broken arm. He's in the operating room now."

"Oh my," she gasped. "Surgery?"

"The doctor said it had to be done to set the break, but it wouldn't take long. But I'm not schur we'll be coming home tonight."

He heard Mary's voice in the background.

"Mary wants to talk to you. Here," she said and put her on the phone.

"Daed? Is Samuel allrecht?"

"He's doing fine. They're fixing his arm."

"Then you're coming home?"

"I'm not schur," he said. "They haven't told me if we can do that tonight. So you be *gut* for Ruby if we have to stay, allrecht?"

It broke his heart when he heard her begin to cry. "Mary, we'll be home soon as we can. Now let me talk to Ruby again."

"I love you. Tell Samuel I love him too."

"I will. I love you too."

He heard Ruby reassuring Mary before she got back on the line. "Mary and I fed and watered the horses," Ruby told him.

"That's *gut*." He hadn't even thought about them.

"Daniel."

"Ya?"

"I'm so sorry. This is all my fault."

Daniel could hear her crying. "Ruby, what's this about?"

"If I hadn't scolded Samuel for ruining Mary's cookies, he wouldn't have run out into the road."

"Ruby, you're not responsible for him running out into the road," he said firmly. "He knows better."

He could hear her sniffling. "But—"

"I don't want to hear any more of this. And as soon as we come home, Samuel will say the same thing. Now, are you schur you don't mind watching Mary if we don't get to come home tonight?"

"Of course not. See you when you get home. And Daniel?"

"Ya?"

"I'm glad Samuel's going to be allrecht."

"Danki. Me too."

An hour later, a nurse came to tell him that Samuel had done well in surgery and was in the recovery room. "I'll let you know when he's in a room," the nurse told him.

Daniel felt weak with relief. "Danki for coming to tell me."

As promised, she came for him when Samuel was put in a room in the pediatric section. Samuel looked pale, but the nurse checking his blood pressure smiled and said he was doing fine.

"He may not wake until morning," she said. "Parents are welcome to stay."

Daniel sank into the recliner next to the bed. Its padded cushions felt *gut* after hours of sitting in the waiting room.

The doctor came in a few minutes later, still wearing his scrubs. "Surgery went well. I do want Samuel to spend the night for observation. We haven't seen any indication of internal injuries, but it's best to be cautious."

Daniel felt his stomach lurch. "Internal injuries."

"Like I said, we haven't seen any sign of that. Samuel was pretty lucky to just be banged up a little and have a broken arm."

He nodded and silently thanked God. "Whatever you think is best."

The doctor shook his hand. "Hang in there. I'll be back in the morning. The nurses will give you my number if you have any questions."

"Did you get something to eat?" a nurse asked him when she came in to check on Samuel.

He shook his head.

"You drink enough of that waiting room coffee, and we'll have to get *you* a bed. Let me see if we have anything we can offer you."

"I don't need anything. I don't want you to go to any trouble."

"It's no trouble. We try to keep something for parents," she told him. "We know they won't leave their children to take care of themselves."

She left, and when she returned, she had a plastic-wrapped ham and cheese sandwich, some fruit, and a carton of milk. There was a cup of apple juice for Samuel for when he woke up, but the nurse advised him not to share his food with Samuel because he'd probably feel nauseous for a while after surgery.

"It's best to let his stomach settle down," she said.

Daniel ate the sandwich and fruit and drank the milk. And then he leaned back in the chair, used the lever to raise the footrest, and closed his eyes.

CHAPTER SEVENTEEN

Ruby did everything she could think of to relieve one worried little girl's mind.

But all Mary wanted to do was sit and stare at her Dat's cell phone as if she could make it ring by the intensity of her doing so. They did some weeding in the two kitchen gardens, and Mary still looked anxious and restless.

"I'm not schur your Dat will call again," she warned Mary. "He'll be busy helping take care of Samuel. Let's make supper. If your Dat and Samuel come home this evening, they'll be hungerich."

So they made supper, and after it appeared that it would just be the three of them, Mary was persuaded to eat. After they cleaned up the kitchen, they went over to Mary's house, checked on the horses, and fed them some apples. Then they went into the house and got Mary a nightgown and clothes for Schul the next day.

"Just think—you can have a sleepover with us if they're not home at bedtime," Ruby told her as they chose a favorite book and then left the house and locked up. "I used to love having sleepovers at Leah's house."

Mary smiled politely, but Ruby could see she didn't seem enthusiastic about the idea.

Back at Leah's house, they went upstairs, and Ruby started water running in the tub, adding some bubble bath when Mary mentioned she liked it. Mary didn't stay in it long, though, and immediately asked if her Dat had called when she got out.

"I'm schur everything's allrecht." She led her into her room and sat on the twin bed Mary would use that night. "Komm, I'll brush your hair for you."

Mary sat obediently on the bed beside her, and Ruby undid the braids they'd pinned up for her bath. "Mamm used to brush my hair before I went to bed." Her lower lip quivered. "I don't want Samuel to be dead!"

Ruby hugged her. "Samuel's going to be allrecht. It takes time for the doctor to help someone, that's all."

"They couldn't help Mamm." Mary pressed her face against Ruby's chest and began weeping.

Ruby didn't know what to say, so she just held her. She prayed and then jerked when Daniel's cell phone rang. Snatching it up, she listened to Daniel telling her Samuel was out of surgery and going to be allrecht but that they'd have to stay the night.

"Here, Mary wants to talk to you," she said and handed the phone to her.

It took a few minutes, but finally, Mary handed back the phone. She looked resigned. She had wanted her Dat and Samuel to come home that night but didn't cry or pout, and for that Ruby was grateful.

"So we'll see you in the morning," Ruby told Daniel. "Try to get some sleep."

She tucked Mary into bed, and they said good night to Leah when she came upstairs and paused at the door to say she was going to have an early night and read in bed. Ruby went downstairs to fix herself a cup of tea. It was too early for her to go to bed, and besides, she didn't think she was going to find it easy to sleep that night.

Taking the tea into the living room, she chose a book from the bookcase and settled into the recliner.

And despite the fact that she thought she wouldn't be able to sleep, she fell asleep in the chair. She woke, startled, to find it was morning, and someone was banging on the front door.

When she opened it, she saw Isaiah standing on the porch.

"What are you doing here?" she asked, trying to cover her mouth as she yawned.

"I left two messages for you on Leah's answering machine," he said, looking unhappy. "Why didn't you return my calls?"

"I'm sorry. I didn't check the machine yesterday. We were a little busy. Samuel got hurt and—"

"I heard."

"You heard?"

He nodded. "Amish grapevine. My Mudder told me when I got up this morning. So, do you want to go to breakfast?"

She shook her head. "I can't. I'm watching Mary until Daniel gets home from the hospital. I need to get her up and walk her to Schul. Besides, don't you need to get to work?"

He shrugged. "I'll get there when I get there."

She raised her brows. His Dat wasn't going to be happy about that. "Well, maybe some other time."

"I'll stop by after work, see if you want to do something then."

Ruby started to say something, but she heard Mary calling her. "I have to go. Have a *gut* day."

As she walked to the kitchen, she frowned, remembering that Isaiah hadn't asked how Samuel was doing.

Mary didn't want to go to Schul and tried to talk Ruby into letting her stay until her Dat got home but finally agreed to go when Ruby told her she'd ask Daniel to pick her up early. Ruby changed, then fixed her breakfast and walked her to Schul.

Teacher Lovina welcomed Mary with a hug. Like Isaiah, she'd heard about the accident. They went inside, and Ruby walked home.

A van was pulling up in front of Daniel's house just as Ruby got to Leah's. She hurried over to see Daniel paying the Englisch driver. Then he reached inside, and when he turned, he held Samuel in his arms.

"I'm so glad you're both home!"

Daniel smiled when he saw her. "I didn't get to call you before we left."

"I just walked Mary to Schul. She was worried about Samuel and didn't want to go, but I told her you might get her early, and she went without a fuss."

"Danki."

Samuel looked pale and avoided her gaze. He had a bulky white cast on one arm and scrapes all over his skinny legs.

She followed Daniel up the walk to his house. "Have you had breakfast?"

Daniel set Samuel down so that he could unlock the door and open it, then picked him up again and carried him inside. "Nee. We went down and waited for the driver."

"Let me fix you something. Samuel, what do you want for breakfast?"

He shrugged and still wouldn't look at her. Ruby watched him trace a finger over the signatures she saw on his cast.

"Samuel." Daniel's voice was quiet but firm as he set the Bu in a chair at the kitchen table.

"Scrambled eggs, please."

"Scrambled eggs it is. Daniel? You too? And some coffee?"

"That sounds great. Especially the coffee."

She filled the percolator and started the coffee first. She hadn't cooked in Daniel's kitchen before, but it was easy to find what she needed. In no time, she was stirring the scrambled eggs in a skillet and warming up some cinnamon rolls she found in the bread box.

The room was quiet as the two sat at the table. Daniel looked exhausted as she set a cup of coffee before him. She poured a glass of orange juice for Samuel, and her heart ached as he avoided her eyes again.

"I'm sorry I scolded you," she told him, blinking back tears.

"Ruby—"

"It was my fault," Samuel said, cutting off his Dat's words. "I shouldn't have done that to Mary. I'm sorry for all the trouble I caused." He began crying.

"Oh, Samuel, don't cry, don't cry," Ruby murmured as she bent to hug him. "Just don't ever run out into the road like that again. Promise?"

He leaned his head on her shoulder and nodded. "I won't."

She waited until he lifted his head, reached for a couple of paper napkins, and wiped his damp cheeks. "Now eat your breakfast. You can tell Mary you're sorry when she comes home from Schul." She looked at Daniel. "I should go."

"Stay," he said.

She hesitated but then sat at the table with them while they ate.

Daniel saw that Samuel was asleep in his arms before he bent and laid him down in his bed.

Samuel had been nodding off over his breakfast, and seeing he'd eaten most of it, Daniel had picked him up and carried him upstairs. When he came down, Ruby was clearing the table. He walked over to the stove and poured himself another cup of coffee.

"Mary didn't want to go to Schul," she told him. "She was really worried about Samuel. Said"—she paused, then took a breath and went on—"she was afraid he wouldn't come home like her Mudder never came home."

He winced. "I had some bad moments when we got to the hospital. When I walked into that emergency room last time, it was too late. Sadie was already gone."

"Daniel, I'm so sorry. For Sadie and for what you went through when you went to the hospital this time."

"Danki." He found the compassion in her gaze helped a lot. "I've been lucky one of Samuel's pranks hasn't landed us there before this. The nurse who took the information about his medical history said her Sohns make regular visits."

He set his cup down. "I'm glad you told me about Mary. I should go pick her up and bring her home. I'll call my Mudder and see if she can watch Samuel here so that I can do that."

"Oh, I almost forgot to give you back your cell phone." She pulled it from her apron pocket and handed it to him. "But there's no need to call your Mudder. I can stay while you get Mary."

"You've already done enough—"

"I've done little. And it won't take long. Go."

So he found himself thanking her again and heading out to get Mary. He was glad he did when she looked up as he opened the door to the schoolroom and jumped up to run to him.

"Where's Samuel? You said he was allrecht!"

"He is. He's home sleeping. I came to get you because Ruby said you were worried."

Mary threw her arms around him and clung to him. Teacher Lovina walked over to him.

"May I take her home early?"

She nodded and smiled. "Mary told me what happened. I'm glad Samuel's allrecht. We'll see you tomorrow, Mary. And hopefully, we'll see Samuel soon."

Mary had what seemed like a hundred questions for him as they walked home, her hand tight in his. He answered them all, and she finally ran down.

"Did you have a *gut* time staying with Ruby and Leah?"

She nodded. "Ruby let me sleep in her room. It's the one she said Leah always had her sleep in when she stayed overnight. It has twin beds. She has this little box she keeps on her dresser. Leah painted her name on it in red, and it has a shiny red stone on it and something about Proberbs?"

"Proverbs. It's a book in the Bible."

"Anyway, she said she never understood why her parents gave her that name. Said Leah told her it's from Proverbs and put that on the box with the pretty red stone."

Daniel remembered the phrase. *Who can find a virtuous woman? For her price is far above rubies.*

He thought it fit her well. When he realized Mary was still talking, he tuned back into her.

"And when I woke up scared in the night, she let me climb into her bed, and she held me." She leaned against him as they walked. "I love her, Daedi. I love Ruby."

"I know, Boppli. I know."

And he knew he did too. But how did Ruby feel about him?

They climbed the stairs to their home, and Mary threw open the door and ran inside.

"Don't wake Samuel if he's sleeping!" he called after her.

"I won't!"

But as he followed her into the kitchen, she raced ahead of him, and her steps on the stairs to the second floor were anything but quiet.

"Mamm!" he said as he realized his Mudder was sitting at the kitchen table, having a cup of tea with Ruby.

Before he could say anything, Ruby was getting to her feet and excusing herself, saying Samuel hadn't stirred and that she'd see him later.

And she was gone.

He sighed inwardly but told himself they'd talk later. Turning, he bent to hug his Mudder. "It was nice of you to come by."

"Well of course I would." She stared at him intently. "How are you doing? Going to the hospital must have been hard."

"Ruby told you?"

She frowned and shook her head. "Nee. I just assumed it would be."

He sat down and sighed. "It was. But I got through it." *Because what other choice did I have?* he asked himself.

"I went up and peeked in on Samuel. He was sleeping."

They heard a thump overhead. "I doubt he still is," Daniel said wryly.

"Let them be. It's probably the best thing for both of them."

He felt her studying him. "What?"

"Nothing," she said with a smile. "I thought I'd see if you needed any help. But it seems Ruby had everything in hand. She was washing breakfast dishes when I got here."

Daniel nodded. "She was outside when we came home and fixed us breakfast." He yawned. "What I'd like most right now is a nap, but that's not going to happen."

"Probably not unless you can convince those two to nap," she told him as they heard another thump over their heads. "But they'll likely go to sleep early tonight if you're lucky. How about if I make something for supper that you can heat up later? I know you need to get started on your chores."

"Best offer I've had all day."

But as he walked out to the barn, he knew that wasn't the truth. The best offer had been Ruby offering to make him breakfast.

The day went by quickly with chores and taking care of a fussy Samuel, who was hurting but didn't want to take medicine for it. Daniel finally disguised the pain pill in a peanut butter and jelly sandwich his Sohn requested for lunch, and soon Samuel stopped complaining about hurting and fell asleep.

Mary conked out as well in the same bed, her arm wrapped around her Bruder. Daniel stood watching them for a long moment, savoring the sweet sight. He figured they'd be back to bickering about something in a day or two. But for now, they were a silent picture of love.

He left them and went downstairs to fix something to eat and found himself dozing at the kitchen table.

Coffee, he told himself. *Have some more coffee.* It wouldn't be long before supper and evening chores; then he could talk everyone into an early bedtime.

He took the cup of coffee out to the front porch and thought sitting down in the rocking chair enjoying a cool breeze was almost as *gut* as taking a nap.

A buggy pulled up in front of Leah's house. Daniel watched Isaiah get out and walk with his usual cocky stride up the path to the steps.

And felt relief when Isaiah returned to the buggy with an unhappy expression on his face—and without Ruby.

CHAPTER EIGHTEEN

Ruby was weeding in the kitchen garden the next afternoon when she glanced over and saw Samuel sitting on the back porch steps of his house.

His thin shoulders were slumped, and he was just staring at his cast. She'd never seen such a despondent little Bu. She stood, rinsed her hands in a bucket of water, and walked over to him.

"How are you feeling today, Samuel?"

He looked up at her from under the brim of his straw hat and shrugged. "Allrecht."

"Where's your Dat?"

"Barn."

"When do you get to go back to Schul?"

Another shrug. "Dunno. Maybe tomorrow. Doesn't matter. Schul's dumb."

"I'll be right back."

She walked to the barn and went inside. Daniel glanced up from mucking out a stall and looked surprised to see her.

"Guder Mariye."

"Guder Mariye. I just spoke to Samuel."

Daniel stopped what he was doing. "He's supposed to stay on the back porch."

"He's still there," she said quickly. "He just looks bored. I thought maybe he might like to come over to the house and do something with me while you do your chores."

"You've done enough."

She shook her head. "Leah's over at my house this morning visiting with my Mudder. I thought maybe Samuel could draw her a birthday card while I work on my quilt."

He rested his forearms, one atop the other, on the handle of the shovel. "Are you schur you don't mind?"

"I promise you I don't. Now, if Samuel doesn't like the idea, then I guess he'll just sulk on your porch steps."

"Allrecht. It'll give me a chance to finish here and then wash up without worrying about him getting into mischief." He walked outside with her and stood at the entrance of the barn, watching as she walked to the back porch.

Samuel agreed to go to Leah's house when Ruby told him that his Dat said it was allrecht. Daniel didn't need to know that it took the mention of root beer and cookies. When Ruby opened the door to Leah's kitchen and glanced back, she saw that Daniel had gone back inside the barn.

She settled Samuel at the table, opened the glass bottle of local root beer, and poured it into a plastic cup Leah kept for young visitors. Then she put a handful of oatmeal raisin cookies on a plate and set it before him.

"I thought you could make Leah a birthday card," she told him. She loved how big his eyes got when she reached into a kitchen drawer and pulled out a giant box of crayons. Then she went to another drawer and found the white and colored craft paper and set a few sheets of each in front of him.

"I have some glitter, but I wasn't schur if you liked it." She held up the bottles of pink and silver glitter.

He wrinkled his nose. "Glitter's for girls." Then, when she went to put it back, he said, "But Leah's a girl. A grown one, right? She'd prob'ly like it on a card."

"You're right." She set it on the table, then got her quilt and sat at the opposite end of the table, far from his artistic endeavors.

They worked in companionable silence until Daniel came in to see if Samuel was hungry and wanted lunch. When he asked if he could have a peanut butter and jelly sandwich, Ruby insisted on making him one.

"What about you?" she asked Daniel. "What would you like?"

"I can go home and make something."

"Don't be silly. It's no trouble. How about ham and cheese?"

He didn't want her to be getting out more sandwich makings and bothering, so he shook his head and asked for the same as Samuel.

She decided it sounded *gut* and fixed herself one as well.

"What's going on here?" he asked as he sat at the table and looked at what Samuel was doing.

"Just doing some drawing and some quilting," Ruby said.

"Ya, just some drawing," Samuel said with more skill at fibbing than Ruby had.

Daniel brushed the dab of silver glitter from his Sohn's nose with his forefinger. "Your nose is shiny."

"It's a secret," he said, swiping at his nose with his fist.

"We can tell your Dat," Ruby told him. "We're making a birthday card for Leah."

Mary came home from Schul and started on a card for Leah as well. She was a little too fond of the pink glitter. Ruby had to hold the card over the garbage can and tap the back of it to discard the excess. Then she saw it had fallen all over her shoes and the floor.

She got out the broom and worked hard to sweep it up, but when Daniel opened the door, the breeze scattered it.

"Let me show you what to do," he said and dampened a paper towel with water from the tap. He bent down and wiped up the glitter, then tossed the towel in the trash. "Done!"

"Daedi knows how to do everything," Mary said with a smug grin.

"We made glitter pinecones for Christmas," he told Ruby. "I learned."

Ruby saw that he had a thin line of glitter under one eyebrow. He must have touched his face as he was helping her clean it up. She opened her mouth to tell him and then heard a buggy pulling into the driveway.

"Quick, hide everything!" she cried, gathering up the supplies. "That's Leah coming home!" She scooped up the cards and thrust them into a kitchen drawer while Daniel and Mary wiped off the table.

When Leah walked in the back door a few minutes later, the Kinna were drawing, Daniel was drinking coffee, and Ruby was standing at the kitchen sink filling a pan with water.

"Well, hello, everyone," she said as she set her purse down on the bench near the back door. "What's going on?"

"Drawing," said Mary.

"Coloring," said Samuel.

"Oh, that's nice." She turned to Ruby. "What are we having?"

Ruby stared down at the pot filling with water. She had no idea. "Spaghetti," she said quickly. She'd need to boil water for that. Now she just had to hope they had everything she needed to make it as she heard the Kinna cheer at her choice.

Leah poured herself a cup of coffee, took a seat at the table, and stared at Daniel as she sipped.

Mary glanced up and began giggling. She poked her elbow into her Bruder's side, and he started to snarl at her before she jerked her head at their Dat. Samuel began giggling too.

"What's so funny?" Daniel demanded.

"I'd have thought you'd prefer the silver glitter to the pink," Leah said calmly.

He rubbed a hand over his face, and sparkles fell onto the table. When he gave her a desperate look, Ruby fumbled for an excuse.

But she just couldn't stop laughing.

Daniel used a paper napkin to wipe the glitter off the table as he grinned at Leah. "I helped Mary with a project earlier."

"Yeah, we—" Samuel stopped abruptly when Daniel gave him a hard look. "We helped her," he said and went back to studiously coloring.

He watched Ruby get a package of hamburger from the refrigerator and brown it in a pan on the stove.

"I need to go down to the basement for the spaghetti sauce," she said, and he saw her mouth quirk with a grin as she passed him on the way.

Well, she could have all the fun she wanted at his expense, he decided. He and the Kinna were getting a supper out of it—and a *gut* one at that.

When she returned with the jar of sauce canned the previous summer, she added pasta to the pot of boiling water and then mixed the sauce into the hamburger. Soon, delicious scents filled the room.

Daniel heard his stomach growl and hoped no one else did. All he'd had for lunch was a peanut butter and jelly sandwich with Samuel. That hardly filled a man who'd worked at chores all day.

Mary set aside her drawing and got up to set the table without being asked. Daniel felt a quiet pride in seeing her behavior.

"What can I do?" he asked Ruby.

"Hmm?" she turned from the stove. "Oh, you could get the salad I made earlier out of the refrigerator. And the pitcher of iced tea."

"I can help," Samuel offered.

Ruby smiled at him. "Maybe tomorrow. That arm looks like it's hurting you."

Daniel frowned, thinking he should have noticed. He pulled out the bottle of prescription painkillers and fetched a glass of water for Samuel to take one.

Leah rose, took a loaf of bread from the bread box, carried it back to the table with a cutting board and knife, and began slicing it.

"Your Mudder and Dat said for me to say hello," she told Ruby. "I think they miss you."

"I'll go see them soon," she said as she set a big bowl of spaghetti on the table, then set another of rich red meat sauce beside it.

Daniel said the blessing over the meal and then fixed his Sohn a plate. As they ate, Daniel felt himself relaxing. He hadn't realized until now that he had been wound up by all the tension of the accident and the hours of anxiety and sleeplessness at the hospital.

All felt well in his world with those he loved safe and sound in the room.

Samuel wasn't the only one struggling to stay awake after the heavy meal. Leah invited Samuel to go to the living room with her and said she'd read him a story. They went off to the other room, talking about the hospital.

Ruby insisted she and Mary would take care of the dishes so that Daniel could do his evening chores in the barn. Daniel didn't argue with her. He'd make it up to her somehow tomorrow when the Familye surprised Leah with a birthday supper.

Daniel did his chores as quickly as he could, and when he returned to Leah's, Ruby and Mary were finishing up the dishes, so he went into the living room to get Samuel. He found his Sohn curled up on Leah's lap. Both were sound asleep. He bent to pick up the storybook that had fallen on the floor and set it on the bookcase.

"Time to go home," he whispered in Samuel's ear, trying not to wake Leah. But she stirred and opened her eyes.

"So nice to hold a Kinner," she murmured. "They grow up so fast. Seems like just yesterday I held Ruby like this and read her a story."

"You look tired."

She shrugged. "I probably shouldn't have stayed so long at my Schweschder's today."

Samuel woke and blinked sleepily at him. "Daed."

"Let's go home and get some sleep."

He nodded and slid off Leah's lap. Then he turned and hugged her, careful not to knock her with the arm that was in a cast. "Danki for reading me a story."

She smiled. "I love you, Samuel. I hope your arm feels better really fast."

"I love you too."

Daniel bent to kiss her cheek. "And I love you, Leah. Sleep well."

"You too."

He thanked Ruby for supper when he and Samuel walked into the kitchen. "Sorry you got backed into making us supper," he told her quietly. "Well, actually, I'm not." He grinned.

"Me either." She glanced toward the living room, obviously making schur Leah wasn't coming in. "See you tomorrow."

When they got home, Mary headed to the bathroom to take her bath, but Daniel decided Samuel could skip a night and tucked him into bed.

"We get to surprise Leah tomorrow?" he asked and yawned.

"We do. Remember, it's a secret. You can't say anything if you see her. Or tell anyone."

"I won't." He yawned again.

Daniel kissed his cheek. Samuel was asleep before he pulled the sheet up over his shoulders.

He went back downstairs and made schur the windows and doors were locked. He thought about starting a pot of coffee and decided he'd rather just head to bed as soon as Mary was out of the tub and in her room.

Sad state of affairs when you were ready for bed at the same time as your Kinna, he told himself as he went into his bedroom.

"I'm going to bed, Daed," Mary said as she came into the room. She hugged him. "I'm glad we're all home."

He felt her trembling and sat down on the bed to cuddle her. "Samuel's going to be fine. The doctor told me Kinna heal fast."

"He did?"

"He did. Now, komm—let's get you in bed."

He smiled when she took his hand, and they walked to her room. Lately, she'd been telling him she was too old to be tucked in.

He drew the sheet up over her shoulders, kissed her, and told her he loved her, then left the room.

And thanked God for his Kinna safe under his roof as he climbed into his bed and closed his eyes.

CHAPTER NINETEEN

Ruby woke early and tiptoed downstairs to make breakfast the next day.

She had blueberry pancakes and bacon and coffee ready when Leah came down.

"Happy birthday!" Ruby told her and gave her a hug.

"Danki. My favorite breakfast," Leah murmured as she took her seat at the table. She made a sound of pleasure as she spotted the birthday card waiting for her on the table.

"I know." Ruby set the plate and a cup of coffee in front of her. "What kind of cake shall I bake you?"

She got the predicted response. "I don't want a fuss."

Ruby hid a smile. Her Mudder was baking the birthday cake. "Cookies, then. It's a nice cool day to bake some."

"Fine. Cookies, then."

"Chocolate chip with walnuts?"

"Sounds *gut*."

They spent a quiet morning working on their quilts. Gideon and Daniel both stopped in to wish Leah a happy birthday and have coffee with her. Ruby had asked Daniel to invite Gideon to the surprise Familye celebration later but figured if they didn't all say happy birthday during the day, Leah might get suspicious.

After lunch, while Leah napped, Ruby gave the house a last polish and then went out to the phone shanty to call her Mudder and make schur the Familye was coming as planned.

"I made Leah's cake this morning," she told Ruby. "It's been hard to keep your Dat from trying to cut a piece of it."

"Tell him to keep his fingers off!" Ruby said with a chuckle. "I'm about to bake some butterscotch cookies. If the cake arrives intact, he can take a dozen home."

"They're his favorite. I'll tell him. See you at five."

She hung up and went back to the house to bake. By the time Leah came downstairs, she had chocolate chip cookies, butterscotch cookies, and snickerdoodles in progress.

"My, you'd think it was Christmas," Leah said as she filled a tea kettle with water and set it on the stove to boil.

"Which one would you like to try first?" Ruby asked as she transferred warm snickerdoodles to a cooling rack. "Wait, on a birthday, you should get to try all three."

Leah laughed. "You're too *gut* to me."

Ruby blinked hard so that she wouldn't cry. "That's not true."

Daniel came by a few minutes later. His eyes widened when he saw the cookies on the counter.

"You have great timing," she told him. "Have some. Just be careful—they're hot."

Leah picked up her basket of sketching supplies. "I think I'll sit outside and sketch for a bit. It's such a beautiful day."

Daniel waited until she was outside before he turned to Ruby. "Do you think she suspects anything?"

She shook her head. "I gave her my birthday card at breakfast instead of saving it for later. And when I said I wanted to bake a birthday cake, she insisted she didn't want me to bother. That's why I made cookies."

"But so many." He picked up another and began eating it.

"Won't be if you keep this up," she told him wryly.

"Are you busy tomorrow evening? I thought we could go into town, have pizza or something."

"I'd like that." The oven timer dinged, and she slid on mitts to pull two trays of cookies out and put them on top of the stove. "That's the last batch. Now time to start supper. Mamm is bringing the cake she baked."

"You schur I can't bring anything?"

She smiled at him. "Just the Kinna and the presents we bought that day in town."

"Allrecht." He swiped one more cookie and headed out the door.

Ruby was glad Leah was enjoying herself sketching. It kept the older woman from asking why Ruby was making two large meatloaves for supper. By the time Leah came into the house for a cold drink, they were in the oven, along with potatoes and carrots.

"What a lovely sketch," Ruby said as she glanced at the sketch pad Leah set down on the table.

"Butterflies have always been a favorite," she said as she sipped a glass of iced tea. "They remind me how short the time can be with the people we love. Seems like one visits whenever I sit outside and think of Eli."

Leah finished her drink, picked up the sketch pad, and started for the back door, leaving Ruby standing at the stove, thinking about what she'd said. She knew her Aenti had been feeling more tired than usual lately but hoped that didn't mean she was ready to be with God.

They heard a buggy pulling into the driveway. Leah glanced back at her. "Are we expecting someone?"

Ruby just smiled as her Eldres and Schweschder came in talking all at once, all bearing food and gifts. Right behind them were Daniel, Mary, and Samuel. Gideon walked in a few minutes later.

"What's all this?"

"It's a surprise!" cried Samuel. "Happy birthday!"

"I told you, no fuss," Leah chided Ruby.

"You deserve it after all you've gone through lately," she insisted.

They feasted on all the food, and when Miriam lit the candles on the cake, Leah burst into laughter. "Careful, we'll burn the place down!"

But she seemed pleased to have the Familye around her and told Miriam it was the best chocolate cake she'd ever baked.

Ruby wasn't schur who was more excited when it came time to open cards or gifts—Samuel or Leah. The birthday cards from the Kinna got opened first, leaving a little scatter of sparkle. Leah pronounced them the prettiest birthday cards ever and hugged Samuel and Mary.

The gifts Ruby and Daniel had chosen from the art supply store were appreciated, as was a shawl Miriam had knit and a wooden frame her Dat crafted for one of Leah's sketches, and Emma had sewn a soft cotton nightgown for summer.

After the lovely meal and gift opening, the visitors began to gather their things and head out, not wanting to tire Leah with their company.

"Remember, we're going into town for supper tomorrow," Daniel told Ruby as Leah and the Kinna walked outside to say goodbye to the Familye. "Just the two of us."

Ruby nodded. "I'm looking forward to it."

The warmth of his smile remained with her as she tackled the sinkful of dishes.

Leah came inside and hugged her. "Let me help. That was a wunderbaar surprise."

"Birthday Maedels don't wash dishes."

"I'll remember you said that when yours comes around."

"You go on to bed. This won't take long."

"I think I will." She kissed Ruby's cheek and headed upstairs.

Ruby washed dishes and daydreamed about going out with Daniel the next evening.

Daniel knew the pizza restaurant the Amish and Englisch locals patronized wasn't close to the elegant restaurant that Isaiah had taken Ruby to, but when she slid into the booth and sat, she sighed and smiled at him. The candlelight here came from a half-melted taper stuck in a Chianti bottle, and the red checkered tablecloth was plastic, not fine linen. Ruby told him she'd looked forward to the pepperoni pizza all day long.

"And they have cannoli for dessert."

"Ya." She beamed. "One of my favorites."

They talked about the birthday party, and he told her how long it had taken Samuel and Mary to wind down from the excitement and go to sleep.

"We should have brought them tonight."

He shook his head and reached for her hand. "Nee." When her eyes widened in surprise at his gesture, he wondered if he'd gone too far to show his feelings.

But then her fingers tightened around his and she met his gaze, and something passed between them.

Their server came and took their order with a minimum of chatter. Too soon, Daniel had to release Ruby's hand. The server brought their pizza, left a pile of napkins, and hurried off.

"I'd like us to date," he said abruptly. He felt relief when she smiled at him and nodded.

They stared at each other so long, the server came back to make schur nothing was wrong with the pizza.

Daniel didn't remember what they talked about as they ate, but he knew he'd always remember the buggy ride home as they held hands. And the kiss before they parted when they got home.

As he unhitched the buggy, Daniel counted the time to summer harvest when they could marry. It wasn't that long off. . . .

He was just leaving the barn when he heard the frantic ring of the bell on Leah's back porch and looked over.

"Daniel! Komm! Leah's sick!" Ruby cried.

He rushed over, and when he went inside the house, he found her kneeling in front of the chair Leah sat on. The older woman was white as a sheet and held one hand to her head.

"Daniel, call 911," Ruby said. "Leah nearly fainted."

"I'm just a little dizzy," she protested. "I'm not going to the hospital. I just need to lie down." But when she stood, she would have slid to the floor if he hadn't caught her.

Daniel lifted her—she seemed to weigh as little as Mary—and carried her to the sofa in the living room. He laid her down carefully, dialed 911 on his cell, and told the dispatcher what she needed to know. Then he turned to Ruby. "Go get her shawl and her purse. They'll be here in a few minutes."

This time he didn't ride in the ambulance as he had with Samuel and had to watch Ruby climb inside. She looked scared, but he knew she'd do what was needed for Leah. He was scared too. Leah had opened her eyes for only a moment as the paramedics put her on a gurney and took her from her home.

Ruby looked surprised when he joined her in the waiting room at the hospital. But when he took her hand, it was cold and trembling, and he knew he'd done the right thing to come. His Mudder had watched the Kinna during their pizza date, and she was more than happy to stay with them so that Daniel could go to the hospital.

"The doctor has already called Leah's specialist, and he says the blood tests show she should probably skip her next treatment, but she just needs to rest more and get her strength back."

"That's *gut*." He felt some relief at the news but couldn't get it out of his mind how frail Leah had looked.

"I called my Eldres and told them they want to keep Leah overnight. Daed wanted to come get me, but I said I wanted to see Leah settled in a room and that I'd call a driver for a ride when I was ready."

"No need. I came in my buggy. I'll drive us home."

The ride home an hour later was a somber one, unlike the earlier trip to town, but they held hands again, and this time when they parted, he hugged her and reassured her that Leah would be allrecht.

"I know you're going to say she's a strong woman," she said, obviously fighting tears.

"You'll see I'm right," he insisted.

And he was.

Leah came home bright and early the next morning, and he watched her walk without assistance into her home.

He checked on her for the next several days and saw that she was getting stronger. Ruby admitted he'd been right about Leah being strong but still worried and fussed over Leah until the woman pulled Daniel aside and begged him to take Ruby for a drive so that she'd get some peace.

"I heard that," Ruby said as she stood at the stove, stirring a pot of soup.

Samuel came in the door, bearing a bunch of flowers he'd picked from the front yard. "These are for you and Leah," he said, holding them out to Ruby.

Daniel hid his grin as she thanked the boy, but as she hugged him, she looked over the flowers as if she suspected a prank. She filled a vase with water and arranged them, then set them in the center of the table before Leah.

"Let's all go for a drive and get ice cream," he suggested.

Samuel gave a whoop of joy, and Daniel sent him off to get Mary.

"I don't think I should leave Leah," Ruby said, biting her lower lip.

"I'm not a Kinner," Leah told her tartly. "Besides, your Mudder is coming over in a bit. She'll fuss enough over me without you being here."

"Well, then, if you insist."

"Don't take offense. I'm fine. I think I'll sit in my recliner and sketch. Bring me back some butter pecan."

Ruby sighed and hugged her. "I will." She gathered Leah's sketch pad and the box of pencils she used and took them into the living room to set beside the recliner. Once she saw Leah safely ensconced in the chair, she nodded and walked back to the kitchen with Daniel.

Then he saw her face contort with pain, and tears slipped down her cheeks. "The last time Leah worked on her art, she sketched a butterfly flitting over a flower and told me butterflies were her favorite to draw because they reminded her of how short the time can be with the people we love. And that often one would visit her when she thought of Eli."

He wanted to offer words of comfort, but before he could, Samuel walked in, took one look at Ruby, and walked back out, slamming the door.

"Samuel!"

Daniel caught up with him outside and grabbed his shirt. "What was that about?"

Samuel stared down at his shoes. "Nothing."

"It's not nothing. Tell me what's the matter."

"I don't like you being mean to Ruby. I love her."

Daniel fought back a laugh. "I wasn't being mean to her. She was feeling sad, and I was talking to her. I love her too."

Samuel looked up at him. "You do?"

He nodded. "And I think she loves me. But it's something we're not ready to tell anyone else yet."

"A secret?"

"Ya. Just for you and Mary and me." *Can this mischief-maker be trusted with such?* he wondered. But he didn't have any choice.

Ruby stepped out. "Is everything allrecht?"

"Ya," he said, holding out his hand. "Let's go get some ice cream." He watched as Samuel gave Ruby a grin and then raced off, yelling for Mary.

"What were the two of you talking about?" she asked him as they walked over to his barn.

"It's a secret," he told her. And when he glanced at her, she laughed and shook her head.

"There's that look of mischief in your eye that's so much like Samuel. I wonder if I should be worried."

He just grinned at her.

CHAPTER TWENTY

Ruby lost her argument with Leah about attending church.

She should have known she would. Too often, she lost arguments with the strong-willed woman.

"I'm just not schur you're ready to attend," she told Leah as they ate breakfast. "I think we should both stay home."

"And I say we're both going." Leah finished her coffee and looked at Ruby. "Now, are you going to go hitch up the buggy, or shall I?"

There was no way Ruby was allowing her to perform that chore. She put her dishes in the sink—no time to do them now, after they'd had their argument—and went out to the barn.

When Leah had to sit on a hard bench for three hours for the church service, she'd see that she wasn't strong enough.

"Then we'll get her to come home and rest," she told Ned, and he snorted and nodded his big head as if he agreed with her.

After she had the buggy hitched up, she went inside, washed her hands, and got her purse.

"Ready?"

Leah nodded. Ruby smiled and slipped her arm companionably in Leah's as they walked out together. Ruby considered it

Leah's way of accepting help without asking for it or feeling she couldn't make the walk to the buggy by herself.

"Beautiful day," Leah said with a sunny smile as they rode to the Zooks' home, where the service was being held today. "Feels *gut* to be outside." She sighed as she looked out the window. "I can't wait to see everyone."

Ruby felt a stab of guilt. Maybe she was wrong. Maybe it would do Leah more good than bad to get back to her routine. Leah dearly loved church and seeing all her friends.

Daniel was already at the Zooks' home. "Guder Mariye," he said as he helped Leah out of the buggy, then went around to Ruby's side and told her to go in with her Aenti and that he'd take the buggy over to where the others were parked.

"Danki," she said, grateful for the courtesy.

Miriam and Emma were already seated in the women's section and had saved them seats on the bench. Her Mudder leaned over and studied her Schweschder intently. "You're looking much better than the last time I saw you," Miriam told Leah.

"This one is taking *gut* care of me," Leah said as she patted Ruby's hand.

Ruby lifted her eyebrows. Leah was always complaining that she was fussing. Then, when she saw how her Mudder smiled and looked more relaxed, she realized why Leah had said it.

Mary appeared at her side and gave her a shy smile. "May I sit with you, Ruby?"

"Of course." She glanced over at the men's section and saw that Daniel had come in and sat with Samuel. As she did, she caught a flash of movement and saw that Isaiah was sitting a row back from them and was trying to get her attention. She nodded and smiled at him and realized that she hadn't thought about him in days. It gave her a pang of guilt before she told herself that she hadn't heard from him either.

The service started a few minutes later. It was such a comfort to sit and listen to the lay minister and then lift her voice in harmony with her friends in praise of her God. To her right, she could hear Leah's beautiful voice, and to her left, Mary's childish high soprano. It seemed to Ruby that Leah sang with even more joy than usual.

Ya, Leah had been right—coming to church had indeed been a *gut* thing for her today. She not only lasted through the three-hour service, but she wanted to sit and talk with her friends afterward. Ruby went off to the kitchen to help the other women serve the light meal and coffee, satisfied that someone would come to get her if Leah grew too tired.

She was making the rounds of the room with a pot of coffee when Isaiah approached her.

"I haven't seen you in nearly a week," he complained. "And you haven't answered my calls again."

"Sorry, I've been busy taking care of Leah," she told him. "Sometimes I forget to check the answering machine."

He glanced over at Leah, then back at her. "So how's she doing?"

"Better, I think, but I still worry." When she saw her Dat lift his cup to show he wanted a refill, she turned to Isaiah. "I'm sorry, but I need to get this coffee out while it's hot."

"We need to talk."

"I can't now." Was it her imagination, or was Fannie Mae flirting with Daniel? She wondered as she stared at them across the room.

"Ruby?"

Distracted, she looked back at Isaiah. "What?"

"Let me take you to lunch when you're finished."

"I can't. I want to go home and make schur Leah rests."

"Then a drive," he said, giving her a charming grin. "A short drive."

Later, she'd realize guilt had made her agree.

She served coffee and slices of bread with church spread—the peanut butter and marshmallow treat no one ever outgrew—and kept a careful eye on Leah. Finally, the older woman wore down, and they gathered their purses and rode home.

Isaiah waited in his buggy while she went inside with Leah and then returned to unhitch the buggy and put Ned in his stall with fresh water. As she walked to join Isaiah, she waved a hand at her flushed face and thought it would have been nice if he'd taken care of Leah's buggy and horse while she made schur her Aenti was settled in her recliner.

"I can't be gone long," she said as she climbed into the buggy.

"Fine."

But he didn't sound happy about it.

"I guess you have to take care of her."

"Have to?" She turned and stared at him. "I want to, Isaiah."

"Well, schur," he said as they rode along. "I mean, you have to because you're hoping she'll leave you the farm, right?"

"Leave me the farm?"

"She and Eli never had Kinna. Who else is she going to leave it to? The two of you have always been close."

"Isaiah, I take care of Leah because I love her, not for what she can do for me." A feeling of disgust rose up in her. So this was why he had asked so many questions about the farm. Why he paid attention to her.

"Stop the buggy," she said.

"What?"

"I said stop the buggy."

He pulled over. "What's the matter? Are you not feeling well?"

Thunder rumbled. Or was that her temper? She didn't care. "Nee, I'm not feeling well; I'm feeling sick to my stomach." She got out of the buggy and began walking back to Leah's house.

Isaiah pulled up beside her. "Ruby, get inside. It's going to rain."

She glared at him. "I don't care. Go away, Isaiah."

"What? You're mad because I said something about you inheriting Leah's farm? You can't tell me you never thought about it."

"Nee. I never thought about it."

"Allrecht, have it your way!" He called to his horse and drove away, fast. A moment later, she heard his stereo system blaring.

A cool raindrop hit her face, then another. She glanced up at the sky. Oh well, maybe a walk in the spring rain would cool her off before she got to Leah's.

Then she remembered seeing Daniel at church and Fannie Mae flirting with him. Was he any more interested in her than Isaiah had proven to be?

Nee, she wasn't going to think that way. Daniel wasn't like Isaiah in any way. She climbed the steps to the back porch and walked into the kitchen. Hearing voices coming from the living room, she started toward it.

"I really think you should reconsider what we've talked about," Daniel told Leah.

"Things have changed."

"Nee, they haven't."

"But Ruby—"

She stopped when she heard her name.

"I agreed to leave you the farm, and that's the way it's going to be."

Ruby's hand flew to her mouth to hide her gasp. Leah had agreed to leave him the farm? Why?

When she heard Leah say she wanted a cup of tea, Ruby rushed up the stairs to her room and prayed they hadn't heard her. Had Daniel spent time with her and given her attention to get in her Aenti's good graces? Her self-esteem—only recently improved—plunged. She waited until she heard Daniel leave before she went down and let Leah know she was home.

Daniel went home, unhappy with the fact that he hadn't been able to change Leah's mind about leaving him her farm. It no longer seemed right that the agreement they'd made should stay in effect.

He found Mary and Samuel bickering when he walked into his house. He rolled his eyes and wanted to walk out again. No way he wanted to settle an argument.

"Find something to do," he said, and they jumped. They'd been arguing so much, they hadn't heard him come in. "Go outside and play."

Samuel headed for the door.

"Daedi, it's been raining."

He glanced out the window. It had stopped while he was at Leah's, so he hadn't thought about it. For a moment, he considered letting Samuel go out anyway so that he'd get some peace. But one look at the cast, and he changed his mind. Samuel would find a way to get it wet or dirty or both in five minutes flat.

"Get out a game and we'll play," he told Mary.

"Which one?" She poked her head into a bottom cupboard behind the kitchen table. "We have Dutch Blitz, Candyland, Life on the Farm. Oh, and checkers."

"Checkers," he said quickly. The last thing he wanted to do was play a game about life on a farm after arguing with Leah about her farm. Just what was going to happen when Ruby found out?

"Daedi? You ready to play?"

He realized she'd set up the board, and she and Samuel were staring at him.

"Ya, who am I going to beat first?" he asked as he sat at the table.

He told himself not to worry about Leah's farm. She was going to be around for a long, long time. If things kept on as they were, he figured he and Ruby would be having a discussion about a farm—his—and her moving in here after they were married.

"Daedi!"

"What?"

He realized two sets of eyes were watching him curiously. "Sorry, I'm thinking about something. The two of you play the first game, and then I'll play the winner."

They had to immediately bicker over who got red and who got black. It took him threatening to take the game away for them to settle their dispute.

He wasn't surprised Samuel won. Samuel had been *gut* at checkers from the time he sat down for his first game.

Using the excuse that he wanted to start supper, he urged them to play the second game. He looked at the menu on the refrigerator and saw that a chicken noodle casserole was tonight's selection. The recipe was simple and one he'd made many times. He found the container that held baked chicken leftover from the previous night's supper and carried it to the counter. Then he found a big pot, took it to the sink, and turned on the tap. As he waited for the pot to fill, he glanced out the window. He wondered what Ruby was doing right now. He hadn't had a chance to talk to her at church because she'd been busy serving coffee.

Maybe after supper, he'd find some excuse to walk over to Leah's and see her.

He boiled noodles, drained them, and dumped them into a baking dish. A can of chicken noodle soup and a small jar of mushrooms, followed by a quick stir, and the casserole was ready for the oven.

Could he trust the Kinna not to go near the hot oven if he went next door to see Ruby for a few minutes?

His gaze landed on Samuel's cast, and he decided he didn't want to risk it.

Resigned, he sat at the table and waited for his turn to play checkers with the winner.

After supper, he and the Kinna fed and watered the horses. After that, he had to help Samuel take a bath with a plastic bag taped securely around his cast. He didn't want to end up having to take him back to the hospital for a new cast if this one got wet, so he stayed in the bathroom and watched his Sohn like a hawk.

After he scrubbed the tub—Mary didn't have to nag him—he read Samuel a bedtime story while she took her bath.

And before he knew it, a glance at the clock told him it was too late to go visiting. With a sigh, he fixed himself a cup of coffee and walked out to sit on the front porch to drink it.

He wasn't happy that he hadn't been able to talk to Ruby today beyond a quick hello at church, but maybe what he needed to do was think of a way to talk to her about where their relationship was going.

If she agreed to marry him, he wouldn't be sitting here by himself in the evenings much longer. At the thought, a smile stole over his face.

He'd liked being married. A lot. It felt *gut* to have someone to love and feel that love returned. And he'd enjoyed the companionship and support and sharing the joys and pains of Kinna. He knew Ruby loved his Kinna, and they loved her. They hadn't discussed whether she wanted to have more, but that was something they'd talk about. As much as she'd shown she loved Mary and Samuel, he couldn't imagine that she wouldn't want to have more with him. He'd seen her with Aaron, her Schweschder Emma's Boppli, and she looked like she really enjoyed him.

Tomorrow, he needed to spend some time on his farm books and see where he stood. He knew Ruby's Eldres scraped by on their farm, and he wouldn't want them to be burdened by the expense of a wedding. And Leah wasn't in a position to offer financial help to them.

Just as he decided to go on in and go to bed, maybe read a book, he glanced over and saw a light come on inside the downstairs bedroom that overlooked the porch on Leah's house. Then someone came out and sat in one of the rocking chairs. He strained to see who it was, but when he couldn't decide if it was Leah or Ruby, he walked on over.

It turned out to be Leah. She greeted him and gestured for him to sit in the other chair. "Sorry, I guess you thought it was Ruby," she said with a low chuckle. "She went up to her room early. Seems upset but won't talk to me about it."

"I didn't talk to her today—" he began.

"I know who upset her," she interrupted. "She went for a drive with Isaiah." She rocked and stared down at the dark. "Haven't seen him around here for a while, and I don't think we will be."

Daniel watched fireflies dance in the field opposite the house. "I'm going to ask Ruby to marry me," he said, and then he turned to stare at her, shocked at having blurted it out.

He could see her smile in the dim light from the bedroom behind her. "Of course you are."

He laughed and shook his head. "Eli said you were always right."

Leah nodded. "Wise man." After a moment, she laid her hand over his on the rocking chair. "See why it doesn't matter if I leave the farm to you? You'll both share it." She rose. "I'm going to try to sleep. I don't like sleeping down here and not in the room I shared with Eli, but the stairs have been a little difficult the past few days. Ruby doesn't think I know she's been sleeping on the sofa in the living room in case I need her. She sneaks down here late at night and then gets up before I do."

"Nothing gets past you, does it?" he asked with a chuckle.

"Nee."

He rose and kissed her on the cheek, and after he saw the light go out in the guest room, he went home.

CHAPTER TWENTY-ONE

Ruby made coffee and breakfast at the usual time, and when Leah didn't appear, she decided to wait and let her sleep some more.

She sat at the table and sipped her coffee and remembered how she'd walked in the room yesterday and overheard Daniel and Leah talking.

It hurt to think that Daniel might have taken advantage of Leah to get her to agree to that. She didn't want to think a man like Daniel would do that. She'd tossed and turned all night, wondering what she should do. Should she talk to him? To her Eldres? She shook her head and rose. Maybe she should talk to Leah first. She poured a cup of coffee and carried it to Leah's room.

She peeked in and found Leah lying in bed, staring out the window.

"I brought you some coffee, sleepyhead."

Leah smiled and struggled to sit up. Ruby set the mug on the bedside table and rushed to stack the pillows behind Leah to help.

"It's lazy to be in bed at this hour," Leah muttered. "And drinking coffee in bed."

"I call it a treat that's well deserved," Ruby said as she sat on the side of the bed. "Think about how many mornings you rose before dawn and worked for hours before breakfast. Speaking of which, let me go get yours—you can eat it in bed."

"I can get up," Leah insisted.

"Nee, let me bring it in here, and we'll both eat in bed. Remember when I was a little Maedel and wasn't feeling well, and you brought a tray into my room and we ate in bed?"

"I do remember," Leah said with a smile. "You insisted your teddy bear needed his own piece of toast."

"Then you had to wash Teddy because he had jelly all over his mouth."

Leah sighed. "Oh, I hate the way I'm feeling. I want to get through these treatments and get well. They've been bad enough without thinking about a stem-cell transplant if they don't work." She looked at Ruby. "I was reading my Bible last night, and I was thinking. There is no illness in God's kingdom."

Ruby felt her heart stop, then begin beating again. Her skin was like ice. She forced herself to bend down and kiss Leah's cheek. "I love you. I know how hard your fight has been. Rest, and I'll go get breakfast. We'll eat it right here."

"Are you bringing Teddy?" Leah asked with a grin.

"He's sitting on a shelf in my closet back home. Maybe next time," she said, trying to sound light.

She rushed out of the room, fighting back tears at how pale and low energy Leah looked this morning. As soon as she got some breakfast in her, she was calling Leah's doctor.

When she returned minutes later with the tray, she saw that Leah was lying down, her eyes closed. Well, maybe she needed rest more than food, Ruby thought. She could warm it up and bring it back later. And she was calling that doctor and her Mudder.

But when she walked over to pick up the mug on the bedside table, she saw that Leah wasn't sleeping but had passed into eternal rest.

She didn't believe it at first because she felt Leah's presence so much. She bent to check that Leah was breathing, as she'd learned to do in a CPR class taught at the local fire station. Then she did the chest compressions, to no avail.

"Leah, please don't leave me," she begged.

But nothing worked.

Frantic, she ran to the back porch and rang the bell. When Gideon came running out of the barn, she shouted to him to call 911 for Leah and rushed back inside.

Ruby tried more CPR but could feel the warmth leaving Leah. The front door opened, then slammed, and Daniel came into the room. When he saw what she was doing, he urged her aside and took over. He was still trying to revive her when the paramedics arrived. Daniel then left the room so that they could work on her in the small space, and Ruby stood by the door.

Minutes later, the paramedics shook their heads and told her they were sorry.

Numb, she walked out to the front porch. Daniel stood and looked hopeful. She shook her head and sank down into one of the rocking chairs, wrapping her arms around herself, so cold.

"She's gone."

He closed his eyes, and when he opened them, they were full of tears. "I'm sorry, Ruby. I was so certain she was going to beat the leukemia." He stared down at the cell phone in his hands. "I called your Eldres. They're coming over."

The paramedics came out and spoke with her for a few minutes, then left. Ruby went back inside. Leah looked so peaceful, it didn't seem possible she wasn't just sleeping. She smoothed the sheets around her and sat to wait for her Eldres.

Her Mudder rushed in, her cheeks pale and wet with tears. Ruby rose and hugged her, comforting her. "I'm so sorry, Mamm. She seemed more tired this morning, and I was going to call you and the doctor after I got her to eat breakfast. But when I brought it in for her, she was gone."

Her Dat came in and hugged the two of them.

They took over and called the funeral home to make the arrangements. After the funeral home came for Leah, her Eldres insisted Ruby return home with them. She found she couldn't resist them. Numb, she climbed into their buggy and turned away when she saw Daniel standing on his porch looking at her.

Daniel tried to speak to Ruby, but she wouldn't look at him and mechanically thanked him as she stood with her Eldres at the viewing at Leah's house, accepting the condolences of those who had known and loved Leah.

Nearly everyone from the church attended the service. Leah had been loved and loving, and so many felt the loss. Daniel felt it as profoundly as he had the death of Sadie. Aaron, the lay minister, started the service with a prayer and spoke of Leah's love for her church and her late Mann and all her Familye and friends. And of the farm she and Eli owned and how she had looked forward to working on it every day, right to the end. He didn't speak over-long about her character and faith; those who knew Leah didn't need a reminder or to have her held up as an example. After he spoke of her battle for her health at the end of her life, he quoted from Proverbs, urging those attending to "trust in the Lord with all thine heart; and lean not unto thine own understanding. In all thy ways acknowledge him, and he shall direct thy paths."

Daniel glanced at Ruby and saw a flash of pain cross her face. He knew she had so hoped that Leah would survive her battle and hadn't been ready to lose her. Samuel sniffled and pressed his face against Daniel's sleeve. He put his arm around his Sohn and looked to see how Mary was doing. She sat with her Grossmudder's arm around her and cried like her heart was breaking.

He wished he could protect them from the pain but knew that it was part of life. With loss came a deeper appreciation for all they would experience in their lives.

The members sang the old familiar favorites "Walking with God" and "Take My Hand and Lead Me, Father." The service ended with a prayer, as it had begun, and then a long line of buggies proceeded to the cemetery.

As they rode in their buggy, Daniel asked his Kinna to tell him their favorite memory of Leah. Samuel didn't want to, so Mary started first and said she loved it when Leah would talk about her Mudder and how much Sadie had loved taking care of her from the moment she'd been born.

"And Leah made me this dress, and I love it so much," Mary said as she smoothed the skirt over her knees. "I'm going to wear it forever."

"You'll grow bigger, and it won't fit," Samuel pointed out.

"Then I'll save it for my Dochder when I have one."

"My favorite memory of Leah is when she found out that your Mudder died, and she came over and sat with me and we talked. She helped me so much that first night."

"What did she say to you?" Mary wanted to know.

"Not very much," he remembered. "She listened. Leah just listened. She knew that was more important than the words some would come up with to comfort."

They traveled in silence for a few minutes.

"Leah made me snickerdoodles," Samuel said suddenly. "She asked me what was one thing my Mamm made for me that I loved and missed."

Snickerdoodles. Daniel smiled. It was a nice memory.

He was in a somewhat lighter mood when they arrived at the cemetery, and they walked hand in hand to watch Leah's simple pine coffin lowered into the ground. After a final prayer, they headed over to Sadie's grave. They came here on Sadie's birthday and Christmas and any day the Kinna asked. Those times had grown fewer as they got older and accepted her death more.

"We forgot to bring flowers," Mary said.

Samuel found a patch of dandelions, picked a bunch of the golden-yellow blooms, and laid them on the grave. Mary found one that had already gone to a seed head and, closing her eyes tight, blew on the downy white tufts. Daniel realized she was making a wish. The delicate tufts floated off on the breeze.

Sadie's Eldres approached them. The adults had sometimes experienced some difficulty in talking about their loss. Daniel couldn't imagine what Naiman and Martha felt, losing their only Kinner. He didn't know if he'd survive if he lost one of his. But Samuel and Mary ran unreservedly to them for hugs, and Daniel could see how much comfort Naiman and Martha found in their gesture. The five of them stood there for several minutes and then joined others in leaving the cemetery.

Many of those who'd attended the service and graveside returned to Leah's house and shared memories of her while they ate food they'd brought for the occasion.

And when Ruby continued to avoid his gaze and his attempts to talk to her, Daniel knew something was terribly wrong. This wasn't just her feeling numb from her loss. Every time she looked away, every time she avoided his attempt to talk to her, it felt personal.

Ruby was upset with him, and he didn't have any idea why.

Well, now wasn't the time to confront her and find out. But he would get her alone as soon as he could, and he hoped she would tell him what was wrong.

It seemed like forever before people finally took their empty casserole dishes and platters and said goodbye. But still, too many people were around. Miriam and Emma and his Mudder bustled about, washing and drying dishes, cleaning up, talking quietly.

He watched, helpless, as Ruby climbed the stairs to the bedrooms.

"Daedi, can I go talk to Ruby?" Mary asked him.

"Me too," Samuel said.

Daniel couldn't go up there, but he thought about it. Then he nodded. "Allrecht. But you knock on her door if it's closed, and you ask if you can talk to her. And if she says nee, you come right back down. Understood?"

They nodded and walked over to climb the stairs, and judging by how restrained they acted, he thought they'd do as he'd told them.

He looked around for something he could help with.

"Daniel? Want some coffee?" Miriam asked.

He shook his head. "I'd like to see if Gideon's fed and watered Leah's horses. But Mary and Samuel just went up to talk to Ruby."

"When they come down, I'll send them to you."

"Danki. And Miriam, I'm so sorry about Leah."

She gave him a sad smile. "Danki for all you did for her."

"I loved her," he said simply, and he had to rush off before he cried in front of her and made things worse.

CHAPTER TWENTY-TWO

Ruby had come up to her room because she needed a moment away from everyone. She'd told herself she should pack up the things she'd brought and the wedding ring quilt she was still working on and take them home. But instead, she'd just sat there on her bed, holding the little wooden box that Leah had painted with her name and crying, not just for Leah but for herself.

As she sat in the little room with its simple furnishings and the drawings Leah had given her through the years, she realized she had spent some of the happiest moments of her life here. Soon, she wouldn't be able to come here anymore.

When the knock sounded on the door she'd closed for privacy, she groaned and wanted to tell whoever it was to go away.

"Ruby? May we come in?"

"Mary?" She rose and crossed the room to open the door, praying that Daniel wasn't with her. But Mary stood there holding Samuel's hand, and she couldn't resist them.

"Komm in," she said, and after they walked in, she closed the door again.

She sat on the bed, and Mary took a seat beside her. Samuel chose to sit on the twin bed opposite them.

Both showed signs they'd been crying, but they seemed calmer than they had during the service.

Mary was the first one to spot the suitcase Ruby had set beside the bed. "Are you going on a trip?" she asked.

"Nee. I'm going home."

"You're not staying here anymore?"

"This was Leah's home, not mine, Mary."

Samuel frowned. "Then we can't come to see you here?"

It hit her then. She wouldn't be seeing them every day. She'd come to love these two Kinna . . . Mary, with her sweet, eager-to-learn personality, and funny little mischief-maker Samuel. Perhaps she'd loved them even before she loved their Dat.

Today they'd come to talk to her, and in their innocent, child-ish way, they'd given her more understanding and comfort than she'd gotten from all the adults at the funeral. Both of them had known such loss . . . first their Mudder and now a woman who'd become like a third Grossmudder.

Reeling, she searched for something to say as she saw the two of them look like they were going to cry again. She couldn't tell them that she wasn't going far and that she would come see them or they could come visit her. Who knew when she would be able to look at Daniel again without feeling he might have taken advantage of Leah?

"We'll see each other at church," she told them. "And maybe one day, you can come see me at my house. You know where it is."

Would Daniel let them? she wondered. The memory of how he'd said he didn't want Mary to become attached to her flitted back. And who knew if he wasn't seeing someone? A man who could keep secret what he had gotten an old woman to agree to could be hiding other things as well.

Ruby stared down at the box in her hands. She hadn't expected Leah to leave her or her Familye anything. But it wasn't right that it be taken by someone outside of the Familye.

Mary stroked her back. "I liked staying here when Samuel was in the hospital," she said. "You told me how Leah painted the box." She fell silent for a moment. "When we were going to the cemetery, Daedi asked us what our favorite memory of Leah was."

So Ruby found herself talking about it, about how Leah had invited her to stay in the little room the first time and how much she had loved Leah and Eli. When she was finished, she realized both had sat there without fidgeting—even Samuel, who usually couldn't sit still.

"Danki for listening," she said. They were such dear ones.

"Daedi said Leah listened to him talk for hours and hours the night our Mamm died. He said people need to listen, not tell someone how to feel."

How wise, Ruby thought. She frowned. It seemed so inconsistent for him to say something sensitive and be someone to take advantage of another.

"I told Daed my favorite memory of Leah," Samuel spoke up.

Ruby smiled at him. "What was that?"

"She asked me what my favorite thing was my Mamm made for me. I told her snickerdoodles. So she made them for me whenever I asked her."

Then he reminded her of how she'd helped him make them, and he'd teared up as he sniffed the cinnamon and said it smelled like his Mamm. She sighed. That had been the day she'd seen the sensitive side of him—not just the prankster.

"God sent us someone very special in Leah," she said, rising to wrap a cloth around the box and tuck it into the suitcase.

There was a knock on the door, and then it opened. "Ruby, Daniel is here for the Kinna. Then your Dat and I are ready to go home." She looked at the suitcase. "Do you want me to carry that down for you?"

She shook her head. "I'm sorry, but I didn't get to pack."

"Just take what you need; we can come back tomorrow. Your Dat and I will wait for you on the front porch."

Ruby nodded. "Allrecht." It had been a long, emotional day. And it wasn't over yet. She hadn't told her Eldres about what she'd overheard. Everyone had been grieving too hard.

The Kinna stood and held out their hands. "Walk down with us?"

She hesitated, not wanting to see Daniel. But she couldn't resist them—or figure out how to refuse. She told herself he might be waiting for them out on the porch. . . .

So they walked down the stairs, holding hands, and at the bottom, she saw him sitting at the table. He stood, looking so serious. "Mary, Samuel, go home. I'll be right there. I need to talk to Ruby."

They turned to her to get a hug and then did as he told them. Both of them gave her a sad look over a shoulder as they went out the back door.

Ruby watched them leave and then met his gaze. "I don't want to talk to you. Now, if you'll excuse me, I need to pack. My Eldres are waiting to take me home."

Daniel watched her turn and start for the steps and shook his head. She was *not* going to walk away without him finding out what was wrong. He touched her arm. "Ruby, they've gone. I told them I'd give you a ride later."

She spun around to face him, looking angry. "You didn't have any right to do that!"

"We need to talk."

"I don't want to talk to you. You've gotten what you want. Why would you want to talk to me?"

"Look, I don't know what's going on." Daniel folded his arms across his chest and pinned Ruby with a probing look. "What have I gotten? Other than your cold shoulder since Leah died."

"This!" she said and flung out her hand in a gesture to encompass the room.

"I got the kitchen?"

"You cheated my Familye out of Leah's farm!"

"I did *what*?"

"Don't deny it! I overheard you and Leah talking about the farm just before she died. You only paid attention to me to get in her good graces and inherit the farm."

"That's what you think of me?" His eyes flashed with hurt and anger. "What kind of a man do you think I am?"

"Do you need me to tell you?"

His jaw clenched. "I was friends with your Onkel Eli before he died and promised him I'd look after Leah. I kept my promise. I helped her with the farm, and I gave her money each month so that she never had to worry she'd lose it."

He walked over to the drawer where Leah had carefully written down the bank deposits. Ruby saw row after row of notations of deposits from Daniel Fisher.

"That's why she wanted me to have the farm, Ruby. She was in danger of losing it after Eli died, and she knew your Eldres were having problems of their own and couldn't help her. So I did. I have the agreement she signed at the house too. I can show it to you. Komm."

"I don't—"

He took her hand and pulled her toward the door. "Nee, you want proof? I'll show you, and we'll settle this."

"I won't have you drag me," she said.

"Fine. Then komm."

She followed him out onto the back porch, and it was then she saw the Kinna sitting on their back porch. "Daniel, I don't want to go over there. I can't handle seeing the Kinna sad again today. I just can't."

"Then I'll go get it."

"Nee. Never mind. I believe you."

He looked over at his Kinna. "You two go on into the house and get a snack," he called to them. "I'll be there in a few minutes." He waited to make schur they obeyed him and then turned back to her.

"I wish she'd told you about our agreement, Ruby. I don't like that you thought I would take advantage of Leah. I loved her so much."

She frowned. "There was this one time weeks ago," she said slowly. "Leah had been sketching butterflies as she sat back here, and she wanted to talk about when she'd be gone." She shook her head and pressed her fingers to her trembling lips. "I—I think she tried to, but I stopped her. I got too upset when she started talking about after she died."

He reached for her hand. "She was a matchmaker, Ruby. She talked about you so much after my Fraa died. Then you came to take care of her, and I saw the kind of woman you are. I fell in love with you, Ruby."

Drawing her down to sit in one of the rocking chairs, he kept her hand in his. "I came over and talked to her later that day you overheard us, Ruby. I told her I was going to ask you to marry me. She just smiled and said she knew. And she said that was why I didn't need to worry about her leaving me the farm. We'd both share it."

She stared down at their joined hands.

"I wish she was here to tell you that, but she's not." He squeezed her hand. "Look at me, Ruby."

When she finally did, he looked at her with all the love he had in his heart. He'd given her the words. If she didn't see the love he had for her in his eyes, he didn't know what else to do.

Slowly, she did as he asked, and she must have seen what he wanted her to. Her expression changed from doubtful to hopeful. And he saw love in her eyes shining back at him.

"Marry me, Ruby. Be my Fraa and the Mudder of my Kinna. And warm our home with that big heart of yours."

"Ya, I will," she said breathlessly, and before they could seal the promise with a kiss, she caught a glimpse of movement out of the corner of her eye. A curtain twitched on a window of Daniel's house.

"Look," she whispered, and he glanced over his shoulder.

Two little faces looked out the window, and each wore a big grin.

"Think you can handle my Kinna?" he asked. "Well, Mary's no problem, but Samuel can be such a mischief-maker, as you know."

"He's a handful," she said with a laugh. "But together, we can handle him. And more?"

He held out a hand. "And more. Let's go tell them the *gut* news."

Ruby looked at them and smiled. "I think they've already guessed."

EPILOGUE

Ruby and Daniel walked out of their wedding reception for a few private moments.

It had been a long, joy-filled day, getting married and being with all their friends and Familye, but it felt *gut* to stand, just the two of them, on the back porch of her home and steal a kiss as Mann and Fraa.

The air was warm and scented with flowers. Harvest was over, and it had been a bountiful one for everyone here in their community. Cool weather would arrive soon—winter always came too soon—but everyone would be grateful for a rest of sorts after the long, hard work of planting, nurturing, gathering, and canning.

They could hear all the laughter and chatter of their guests drifting outside through the open windows. Lunch had been served after the ceremony, and all would stay and enjoy the company of each other and eat again at suppertime before they shooed their tired Kinna into buggies and headed home for bed.

"I love you," Daniel told her. "My beautiful Ruby."

She felt beautiful in the dress of azure blue. She'd found the fabric on a shelf in Leah's closet, with a note that it was for Ruby's wedding dress. Ruby remembered how Daniel had persuaded her to go into town with him to pick up a birthday present for Leah. When Ruby had asked Leah if she needed anything picked up, her Aenti had said Lillian would have an order for her. At the time, Ruby wondered if Leah intended to make a dress of the fabric, but she had forgotten about it.

Then, when she and her Mudder had gone through Leah's closet to donate her clothes, they'd found the fabric on a shelf with a note attached. It read, "For Ruby's wedding dress."

Leah had known they would get married.

When she smiled, Daniel asked her why, and she told him.

He nodded. "Remember the day I asked you to marry me, I told you she said she knew we would."

They heard giggles, and when they turned, Mary and Samuel leaned out a window and grinned at them.

"Can I have more cake?" Samuel called out.

"How many slices have you had?" Daniel asked.

"Just one."

"Two," Mary said and got an elbow in the ribs from her Bruder.

"Let him have another," Ruby whispered to Daniel. "A small one. After all, it's a special day for both of them too."

"A small one," he told his Sohn. "You don't want to get sick."

He scampered off, but Mary lingered at the window. Ruby knew what she wanted. She leaned over and whispered in Daniel's ear, and he grinned and kissed her. When they looked back a moment later, Mary was gone.

"Your Dochder was as much a matchmaker as Leah in getting us together," she told him.

A blue butterfly landed on the porch railing a few feet from them.

Ruby's breath caught, and her eyes widened as the butterfly lingered and seemed to return her gaze instead of flitting off to sip at the nectar of flowers blooming nearby.

Ruby wondered if her beloved Aenti had joined them on this, the happiest day of her life, and she turned to smile at Daniel.

"Do you see what I see?" she whispered. "You know how Leah loved butterflies."

He nodded and hugged her.

They lingered on the porch until it finally flew off.

RECIPES

SADIE'S BUTTERMILK BISCUITS

Ingredients

- 2¼ cups all-purpose flour
- 2¼ cups cake flour
- 1½ teaspoons salt
- 1½ tablespoons baking powder
- 1 teaspoon baking soda
- 1 cup butter (very cold)—don't use margarine!
- 2 cups buttermilk
- ½ cup flour (for dusting the pastry mat and dusting while rolling)
- 2 tablespoons butter (melted)

Directions

Preheat the oven to 475°F.

Combine the dry ingredients together in a bowl. Cut in the butter until the mixture is crumbly. Add the buttermilk and mix just until combined. The dough will be slightly sticky.

Turn the dough out onto a floured surface and pat it into a horizontal rectangle that is about 1½ inches thick. Fold the left side of the rectangle over the right side and pat it out into a vertical rectangle. Then fold the bottom half up to the top and press it out into a horizontal rectangle again. Repeat the steps above three times, for a total of six folds. Be careful not to overwork the dough while you are doing this. The folding is what creates layers in the biscuits. Sprinkle a little flour on the layers if the dough starts getting sticky, but just pat gently and handle the dough lightly. After making those six folds, gently pat the dough into a rectangle that is about 1 inch thick. Use a sharp circle biscuit cutter and press down through the dough; then lift up. Do not twist the cookie cutter. Just push down and then pull straight up. Place the biscuits on an ungreased baking sheet. Brush the tops of the biscuits with melted butter.

Bake at 475°F for 5 minutes, then reduce the heat to 425°F (without opening the oven) and bake for an additional 8–10 minutes. Allow the biscuits to sit for 2–3 minutes before serving. Serve warm. Makes about a dozen biscuits.

Buttermilk is recommended for the recipe, but if you don't have any, it's easy to make by putting 1 tablespoon of vinegar in a measuring cup. Fill up the rest of the cup with milk and let it sit for 5 minutes. Now you have buttermilk!

SADIE'S SNICKERDOODLES

Ingredients

- 1 cup unsalted butter (softened)
- 1½ cups sugar
- 2 large eggs
- 2 teaspoons vanilla

- 2¾ cups flour
- 1½ teaspoons cream of tartar
- ½ teaspoon baking soda
- 1 teaspoon salt

Cinnamon-sugar mixture

- ¼ cup sugar
- 1½ tablespoons cinnamon

Directions

Preheat the oven to 350°F.

In a large mixing bowl, cream butter and sugar for 4–5 minutes until light and fluffy. Scrape the sides of the bowl and add the eggs and vanilla. Cream for 1–2 minutes longer. Stir in flour, cream of tartar, baking soda, and salt, just until combined. In a small bowl, stir together sugar and cinnamon. If time allows, wrap the dough in plastic wrap and refrigerate it for 20–30 minutes. Roll into small balls until round and smooth. Drop into the cinnamon-sugar mixture and coat well.

Using a spoon, coat for a second time, ensuring the cookie balls are completely covered. To make flatter snickerdoodles, press down in the center of the ball before placing in the oven. This helps to keep them from puffing up in the middle. Place on a parchment paper–lined baking sheet. Bake for 9–11 minutes. Let cool for several minutes on the baking sheet before removing from the pan.

Up to this point, we've been doing all the writing. Now it's *your* turn!

Tell us what you think about this book, the characters, the town, or anything else you'd like to share with us about this series. We can't wait to hear from *you*!

Log on to give us your feedback at:
https://www.surveymonkey.com/r/LancasterRomance

Annie's FICTION